Alger, Horatio,
1832-1899.

A fancy of hers ;
The disagreeable
woman

HORATIO ALGER

A Fancy of Hers

The Disagreeable Woman

HORATIO ALGER

A Fancy of Hers

The Disagreeable Woman

Two lost novels for adults by the man
loved for his rags-to-riches tales for juveniles

With an Introduction by

RALPH D. GARDNER

VAN NOSTRAND REINHOLD COMPANY
New York Cincinnati Toronto London Melbourne

Library of Congress Catalog Card Number 80-13018
ISBN 0-442-24716-8

Printed in the United States of America
Designed by Joan Ann Jacobus

Published by Van Nostrand Reinhold Company
A division of Litton Educational Publishing, Inc.
135 West 50th Street, New York, NY 10020

Van Nostrand Reinhold Limited
1410 Birchmount Road
Scarborough, Ontario M1P 2E7, Canada

Van Nostrand Reinhold Australia Pty. Ltd.
17 Queen Street
Mitcham, Victoria 3132, Australia

Van Nostrand Reinhold Company Limited
Molly Millars Lane
Wokingham, Berkshire, England

16 15 14 13 12 11 10 9 8 7 6 5 4 3 2 1

Library of Congress Cataloging in Publication Data

Alger, Horatio, 1832–1899.
A fancy of hers; The disagreeable woman.
Includes index.
I. Alger, Horatio, 1832–1899. Disagreeable woman.
1980. II. Title.
PZ3.A395Fan 1980 [PS1029.A37] 813'.4 80-13018
ISBN 0-442-24716-8

To my Partic'lar Friends of
The Horatio Alger Society

CONTENTS

Acknowledgments *ix*

Introduction by Ralph D. Gardner *1*

A Fancy of Hers *21*

The Disagreeable Woman: A Social Mystery *105*

Index *176*

ACKNOWLEDGMENTS

Grateful acknowledgment is expressed to the researchers and scholars—some named in the Introduction, others inadvertently omitted—who tracked minutiae of Alger's life. I especially appreciate the ever-ready assistance of Jack Bales, editor of the Horatio Alger Society's publication *Newsboy*, and Edward T. LeBlanc, editor of *The Dime Novel Roundup*.

HORATIO ALGER

A Fancy of Hers

The Disagreeable Woman

INTRODUCTION

THE CREATION OF THE AMERICAN HERO

For the better part of the past half century, most Americans have associated the name of Horatio Alger with a phenomenon peculiar to this country: a person's rise to success, usually against considerable odds. Pressed for identification, Americans may recall Alger to have been an honest, hard-working lad who became a millionaire or the plucky hero of a long series of adventure tales or—among even more fanciful choices—a pen name of Charles Dickens.

As long as we are setting records straight, Horatio Alger, Jr.—which is how he always signed his name—was the real name of a real person. He was born in Chelsea, near Boston, Massachusetts, in 1832 and died in South Natick, twenty-five miles away, in 1899. He was the author of 110 books, almost all of them enormously popular, fast-paced thrillers that were read, reread, borrowed, and swapped by nearly every boy and many girls who grew up in the United States between the Civil War and the Great Depression.

In 1864, after graduating from Harvard and the Cambridge Divinity School, traveling in Europe, being rejected for Civil War service because of asthma, teaching at a number of schools, and seeing his sentimental poetry (he was a student and disciple of Longfellow during college days) and early fiction printed in a variety of publications, he was ordained as minister of the First Parish Unitarian Church of Brewster, on Cape Cod.

Sixteen months later, accused of homosexual relations with two boys, he was dismissed from his pulpit. This was Horatio Alger's first secret and it deserves clarification.

Evidence of this incident (I'll discuss the issue in detail further on) came to light more than twenty years ago. Since then, the sparse facts have sometimes been overlooked or avoided. Most often, however, these facts were over-sensationalized with added guesswork and innuendo by writers who undoubtedly relished the debunking of a literary marvel whose name had become as familiar a part of our heritage as Fourth-of-July fireworks and apple pie.

During the three decades that followed his dismissal, he wrote stories at the rate of three or four each year. He used heroic, alliterative titles such as *Brave and Bold, Sink or Swim, Strive and Succeed, Strong and Steady, Try and Trust,* and *Fame and Fortune.* His heroes included Frank Fowler, Ben Barclay, Tom Temple, Mark Mason, Paul Prescott, and Ralph Raymond.

Given his own choice, Alger would rather have won his fame and fortune writing fiction for adults. Indeed, that was how his career began. But after the astonishing success of his eighth book, *Ragged Dick,* in 1868, a pattern was set, at least as far as his publishers were concerned. Fearing that his novels for mature readers would disappoint adoring youngsters, they discouraged his efforts or, at best, issued these works anonymously or camouflaged under a pseudonym. The desire to achieve recognition as a writer for adults became the second secret that burdened Horatio Alger throughout his busy, otherwise successful life.

"If *Ragged Dick* Can Do It, So Can I!"

In his many tales for young people, Alger preached variations on the theme that any spunky fellow can whip the town bully; he can eventually rise from newsboy to banker, from farm boy to senator, from railsplitter to president of the United States. Alger's stories for the first time dramatized, at his readers' level, adventurous exploits that teachers recommended, ministers quoted in sermons, and families read in the parlor. Alger's stories were a welcome change compared with the dull, didactic fare and lurid dime novels that were available during post-Civil War days. His books were even preferred to the imported works of Dickens, who did not—as Alger did—lead his characters to high reward; Hans Christian Andersen, whose stories seemed too melancholy for youngsters; and the Brothers Grimm, whose characters often were frightening to children.

What was the Alger formula? Let me give you this capsulized tale:

His hero was about fifteen years old, usually an orphan. In some instances, he might have been a country boy whose family lost—or was about to lose—their little farm to the unscrupulous village squire; or a ragged urchin who does not know where he came from. In any case, after a few pages he was adrift on the streets of Lower Broadway with only a few cents in his pockets. But he was ambitious and took up some menial line of work: bootblack, newsboy, or messenger.

From the beginning—sometimes from the first sentence—he had enemies, occasionally a scurrilous, drunken, ex-convict stepfather. There was the swaggering snob who despised him and conspired with other evildoers, among whom we found the scoundrel who swindled the hero out of his birthright and went to such measures as slugging, kidnapping, or shanghaiing to keep the hero from discovering this crime. There were false accusations and he was occasionally thrown into an abandoned well. More than once he was framed and arrested. Meeting adversity head-on, the hero got out of every scrape.

Before many chapters passed, the youth performed a brave deed, pulling a child or elderly person from the path of an oncoming vehicle or stopping a runaway horse. He jumped into the East River to save a life or flagged down a speeding train to prevent a crash. He also returned many lost wallets and a lot of jewelry.

In appreciation he got a better job, perhaps as a clerk, and was also given a cash reward which he wisely invested in real estate or Erie Railroad stocks. At this point he met his benefactor's daughter, who found him fascinating.

Because he showed initiative and shrewdness, he was sent on a confidential, perilous assignment, giving him the chance to travel, display clever detective work, and get into more hazardous predicaments and escapes. This mission always was a coup and in its course he discovered some secret that cleared up the mystery of his own identity or accidentally met the man who could help recover his legacy. He returned, was warmly greeted by his employer's winsome daughter, and readers began to suspect a romance.

In almost every instance the hero was well on his way to wealth—or, at least, middle-class respectability—by the time he reached eighteen. Then followed the inevitable happy ending with the old homestead saved and the enemy scattered in disarray.

What was the magic appeal of Alger's stories? True, they represented a fixed world of opportunity, security, and eventual prosperity. But more than this, youngsters of those days found them believable. They identified with the hero. Farm lads who rarely traveled a dozen miles from home loved these adventures in the teeming metropolis. City children crossed the Great Plains and Rocky Mountains (as Alger himself did in search of material), taking the overland route to the California gold fields.

These tales were definitely robust, the author inventive enough to inject a bit of the devil into many of his stalwarts. They smoked penny cigars, guzzled whiskey at three cents a shot, and attended Bowery theaters. One hero was presented as *The Bully of the Village* and another was introduced as a burglar entering the Madison Avenue town house of a wealthy old gentleman who, at the story's end, turns out to be his grandfather.

Of course, the heroes' flaws were quickly overcome. The boys reformed, studied nights, and became determined to better themselves. Each story's attraction was in the reader's own resolve: "if *Ragged Dick* can do it, so can I!"

Alger's Influence

But there were carpers who claimed that Alger misled youngsters, probably causing many who stood up to the neighborhood bully to wind up with a bloody nose. Paul Gallico wrote that Alger so frightened readers with tales of evil squires foreclosing the mortgage on the old homestead that millions of Americans grew up fearful of mortgages, though they did not really know why or of what they were afraid.

As the influence of Alger's writing increased, his publisher, A. K. Loring, proclaimed him to be "the dominating figure of the new era. . . . He has captured the spirit of reborn America. The turmoil of the city streets is in them. You can hear the rattle of pails on the farms. Above all, you can hear the cry of triumph of the oppressed over the oppressor. What Alger has done is to portray the soul—the ambitious soul—of the country!"

Innumerable leaders in many fields once read Alger, believed in him, and credit him with providing incentives to try harder. Benjamin Fairless, who rose from being a part-time schoolteacher to become the head of United States Steel, read Alger in his youth. Former New York Governor Alfred E. Smith bought these novels with spare dimes when he was a newsboy on Manhattan's Lower East Side. Carl Sandburg recalled reading shelves of Alger books at the public library near his boyhood home at Galesburg, Illinois, and former Ohio Governor Michael V. DiSalle—himself an Alger collector—believes that "the Alger theme did have a great deal to do in establishing a pattern in my own mind."

In connection with my researching the biography *Horatio Alger; or, The American Hero Era* (Wayside Press, 1964; reissued by Arco Publishing, 1978), the late Archbishop of New York, Francis Cardinal Spellman, told me that as a boy he regularly sought Alger stories at the Whitman, Massachusetts, Public Library. "I read all that were available," he said, "and enjoyed and, I am sure, benefitted from reading them."

Former Postmaster General James A. Farley, who became Board Chairman of Coca Cola Export Corporation, was an Alger reader; so were Joyce Kilmer, Ernest Hemingway, F. Scott Fitzgerald, New York Giants' Christy Mathewson, and Knute Rockne of the University of Notre Dame.

Such was Horatio Alger's influence that his name now possesses legendary meaning. It is used as a symbol, a figure of speech. It has a meaning that no other name implies. When Pulitzer Prize-winning *New York Times* writer James Reston noted in a pre-election column that Republicans sought candidates with a "Horatio Alger image," no further explanation was necessary.

America's Best-Selling Author

And his works—occasionally scoffed at today by those who take Alger's relics of a gentler, less sophisticated time much too seriously—have, nevertheless, earned the stamp of approval of the experts. The selection committee for The Grolier Club's monumental 1946 exhibition, *One Hundred Influential American Books Printed Before 1900,* called *Ragged Dick* "sufficiently Grade A" for inclusion alongside *Uncle Tom's Cabin* and *Moby Dick.* Frank Luther Mott, in his *Golden Multitudes* (Macmillan, 1947), also listed *Ragged Dick* among Over-All Best Sellers, and three others—*Fame and Fortune, Luck and Pluck,* and *Tattered Tom* —as runner-up Better Sellers. Both *Ragged Dick* and *Tattered Tom* were again cited in *Peter Parley to Penrod* (Bowker, 1956), Jacob Blanck's respected compilation of best-loved American juvenile books.

Determining how many copies of Alger's books were printed during his long reign as America's best-selling author is impossible because most of his sixty-plus publishers have long since disappeared. Although Alger's popularity waned during World War I, his books remained in print throughout the 1920s. Some available estimates are astounding.

The most inflated guess, provided by Edwin P. Hoyt in *Horatio's Boys* (Chilton, 1974), is an inordinately high "half a billion." Others range from 400 million—which is just as questionable—downward to the 250 million claimed by Quentin Reynolds in *The Fiction Factory* (Random House, 1955); 200 million quoted in a 1964 *New York Times Magazine* article—the identical total suggested by Russel Crouse in his introduction to *Struggling Upward and Other Works* (Crown, 1945). The historian Stewart H. Holbrook, in *Lost Men of American History* (Macmillan, 1958), put their sales between 120 million and 250 million. "Whatever the figure," Holbrook stated, "it was enormous, probably larger than the sales of any other American author."

Lowest numbers were supplied by Frederick Lewis Allen, who, in a 1938 article in *The Saturday Review of Literature,* said "it is safe to guess that the grand total must have been well beyond twenty million copies"; and Malcolm Cowley, who, in 1945, wrote in *The New Republic:* "their total sales may have reached fifteen or twenty million at a generous estimate." Similarly, Mott places aggregate sales at sixteen or seventeen million. But mystery and Western writer Frank Gruber, who was an avid Alger researcher, declared in his *Horatio Alger, Jr.* (Grover Jones Press, 1961) that *one* publisher, "M. A. Donahue . . . probably sold fifty to a hundred million books in their famous ten-cent cloth-bound editions." Even the most conservative of these calculations would be phenomenal!

Comments on the quality of Alger's products are equally divergent. Russel Crouse loved these stories but called them "literary murder." A *New York Times* editorial, stating that his works had "irresistible attractions," called Alger the "Prose Laureate" of tales for young people. But *New York Times'* critic Brooks Atkinson, in his review of my book *Horatio Alger; or, The American Hero Era,* described Alger as a "prodigious hack" and "literary mechanic." Westbrook Pegler denounced his heroes as "sanctimonious little heels," but Heywood Broun called these books "simple tales of honesty triumphant." Stewart H. Holbrook called Alger's output "the most influential tripe ever published in this country." Note that he used the word *influential.* My favorite comment comes from playwright S. N. Behrman in his introduction to *Strive and Succeed* (Holt, Rinehart & Winston, 1967). Rediscovering an Alger story he had cherished years earlier, he simply declared: "I don't know any comparable reading experience. It is like taking a shower in sheer innocence."

THE FIRST SECRET

On Thursday, August 3, 1961, a local weekly, the *Cape Codder,* reported that "More than 300 years of Brewster history are now on microfilm. The ancient and colorful town and church records were shown at an open house last Friday."

The two-column article, headlined: "Horatio Alger Was A Rascal/ Brewster Gave Him The Sack," was barely revealing, as the entire reference to Alger was contained in these relatively antiseptic lines:

"In one account of a church meeting, the dismissal of the later famous writer, Horatio Alger, is recounted. Alger, who was a minister in Brewster from 1864–1866 was forced to resign after the good townsfolk found that his behavior was somewhat irregular. No Rags to Riches for him, so far as Brewster was concerned. Always the masters of understatement, the worthy men who toiled over the records merely indicated that Alger 'hastily left town on the next train [the church record used the word, *tram*] for ports [the record says *parts*] unknown—probably Boston.' "*

*Possibly the earliest—and equally brief—reference to Alger in Brewster's records appeared in the informal history, *Cape Cod's Way,* by Scott Corbett (Crowell, 1955).

Prior to the microfilming, it appears there was little local interest in the century-old event. Since I had been in Brewster researching my Alger biography, it is likely I was among the first to study the First Parish Unitarian Church records. The section pertaining to Alger (including minor inconsistencies of dating, spelling, etc.) is as follows:

November 13, 1864: Sunday afternoon

Voted—To write the Rev. Mr. Alger (who has been supplying the pulpit for several Sundays) to settle over this Society, provided that the terms can be made satisfactory.

November 26, 1864: Saturday afternoon

Voted. The Parish committee engage the Rev. Mr. Alger for one year at a salary of eight hundred dollars ($800.) per annum. In case of any dissatisfaction the Parish is to give Mr. A. three months notice before dismissing him and he is to give the same notice if he wishes to leave.

March 6, 1866: Tuesday afternoon

Voted Not to engage the Rev. Mr. Alger for the ensuing year—
then
Voted to reconsider the foregoing vote
then
voted to adjourn to Tuesday March 13th at two O'clock P.M.

March 13, 1866: Wednesday afternoon

Voted to excuse Tully Crosby from serving on the Parish Committee the ensuing year . . . to excuse Solomon Freeman (same) . . . same for Freeman Cobb (These men were chosen as the Parish Committee at the previous meeting on March 6, 1866)
then
Voted an investigating committee of three to be chosen to investigate Parish affairs and report to the meeting to be held on Monday March 19th
then
Committee reported the names of Elisha Bangs, S. H. Gould and Thomas Crocker as an investigating Committee. who were accepted by the meeting.

March 19, 1866: Monday afternoon at two O'clock

Voted the clerk be requested to amend his record of the 5th vote at the meeting held on Wednesday March 19th, and insert 'to investigate certain reports in relation to Mr. Alger' in place of the to investigate Parish affairs.
Voted to accept and record the report of the investigating committee. Report of Committee—

Introduction

We learn from John Clark and Thomas S. Crocker that Horatio Alger Jr. has been practicing on them at different times deeds that are too revolting to relate. Said charges were put to the said Alger and he did not deny them. He admitted he had been imprudent and considered his connection with the Unitarian Society of Brewster dissolved.
Signed Elisha Bangs, S. H. Gould, Thos. Crocker, Committee
Voted a Committee of three be appointed by the chair to forward a letter in relation to Mr. Alger to the American Unitarian Association. Chair appointed Solm Freeman, Elisha Bangs, and Geo. Copeland on said Committee. The Committee came in with the following letter which was read and unanimously adopted and ordered to be recorded.

Brewster March 19—1866

To the Rev. Chas Lowe,
Sec. of the American Unitarian Association, Boston
Dear Sir

The undersigned a committee of the Unitarian Society in Brewster duly chosen for this purpose, at an adjourned meeting of said society held on this 19th day of March 1866 would represent that it becomes our painful duty to communicate to you and through you to the American Unitarian Association, That Horatio Alger Jr. who has officiated as our minister for about fifteen months past has recently been charged with gross immorality and a most heinous crime, a crime of no less magnitude than the abomnible and revolting crime of unnatural familiarity with *boys,* which is too revolting to think of in the most brutal of our race—the commission of which under any circumstances, is to a refined or christian mind too utterly incomprehensible—

Whereupon the Society, then convened immediately appointed an able committee of the church and society to investigate the case and act accordingly. That Committee forthwith attended to the duty assigned them and now verbally report, that on the examination of two boys (and they have good reason to think there are others) they were entirely confirmed and unanimous in the opinion of his being guilty to the full extent of the above specified charges.

Whereupon the committee sent for Alger and to him specified the charges and evidence of his guilt, which he neither denied or attempted to extenuate but received it with the apparent calmness of an old offender.—and hastily left town in the very next tram, for parts unknown—probably Boston.

Had he remained longer an arrest or something worse might have occurred, we should scarcely felt responsible for the consequences in an outraged community, and that outrage committed by a pretended Christian teacher.

> No further comment is necessary you know the penalty attached to such unnatural crime by human as well as divine ears. Please take such action as will prevent his imposing on others and advise us as to what further duties devolve on us as a christian Society.
> Solomon Freeman, Elisha Bangs, Geo. Copeland Committee
> Brewster March 19—1866
> The above communication was presented by our Comttee, and voted unanimously to accept and adopt the same in the name of the Society
> W. F. Lincoln Clerk S. H. Gould Moderator
> Chose Solomon Freeman, Tully Crosby and S. H. Gould Parish Committee for the ensuing year

It must be pointed out that there exists no record of the above letter ever having reached the American Unitarian Association, nor does the Brewster archive indicate that any reply to the inquiry in the letter's last paragraph was received. Also, the regional publication of that period, *The Yarmouth Register,* although it regularly reported Brewster news, carried neither a report of this inquiry nor of Alger's departure. In the Summer, 1961, issue of *Uniteen News,* a digest-sized periodical of the Junior Fellowship of the Church of the Larger Fellowship/Unitarian/Universalist, its "Men of Influence" feature was devoted to an unsigned, largely inaccurate biographical sketch of Alger. Referring briefly to his period as a Unitarian minister, the writer commented only that parishioners found Alger lacking in sympathy and understanding; that his sermons were dry in content and poorly delivered. The matter covered in Brewster records is not mentioned.

Fact vs. Fiction

I am an old newspaperman and, as great as was the temptation to evaluate this material in my Alger biography—especially as I would have been the first Alger biographer to do so—I felt obligated to put the accusations to normal tests of verification, corroborative evidence, and reliability. This could not be done satisfactorily at that time and—despite much that has by now been written about these findings—no new *facts* to clarify the events of March, 1866 have, to date, been uncovered.

My own efforts to do so have provided only the following:

A former town official of Brewster, requesting anonymity, told me—and later told at least two more researchers—that others in the community believed the charges were "trumped up" by persons who, for whatever reasons, found Alger unsuitable. My own feeling on this opinion is that if they wanted to get rid of their pastor they were able to do so simply by giving him three months' notice as specified in his contract.

My informant further declared that Alger "denied the charges with dignity" and walked out of the meeting; the two boys were unreliable witnesses and the charges were never officially acted upon. This was hearsay evidence that I was unable to corroborate or verify.

I next showed the transcript to churchmen and legal people who suggested that, although one could—and many would—suspect the worst, that record, per se, was inconclusive. Attorneys agreed that not only was the evidence inconclusive, but that anyone making this public during Alger's lifetime could have, himself, faced genuine legal problems.

In a lengthy article, headlined "Horatio Alger Liked in Natick," in the *Boston Herald* datelined South Natick, Jan. 17, 1949 and signed by staff writer Ken Crotty, Miss Mabel Parmenter, of the local historical society, told Crotty that when Alger arrived there for vacations every summer "there were always two or three young guests coming on with Horatio from New York." She told of "the hikes along the Charles River that Horatio planned for the young boys of South Natick," and that her father "refused to allow her brother to accompany Horatio on these trips" because his "reputation as the country's most popular author of boys' stories did not alter the fact for many people that he had given up his calling as a Unitarian minister after only two years to follow the more worldly life of a literary man."

Miss Parmenter was not available when I arrived at South Natick, but two other lifelong residents told me, almost word for word, the same story. Another was more to the point.

"I suppose you know," she remarked, "that Horatio was a homosexual."

"How do you know that?" I asked.

She explained that on summer evenings, with his brother-in-law Amos Parker Cheney, Alger would take an after-dinner stroll to the Bailey House to relax on the veranda and visit with neighbors and friends. A new waitress at the hotel, recently arrived from Brewster, asked: "Isn't that Rev. Alger?" Told that it was, she disclosed the events she had heard about during her childhood, years earlier.

That was how the news reached South Natick.

Some Opinions, Guesses, and Judgments

In *From Rags to Riches* (Macmillan, 1963), John Tebbel described Alger's association with Charles O'Connor, superintendent of the Newsboys' Lodging House, where, over many years, Alger found material for his newsboy and bootblack stories: "His friendship with O'Connor was a closer relationship than any he ever enjoyed. While it is dangerous to read into it more pathologic tones than may have existed, there were strong elements of the homosexual in this friendship." Although Tebbel concluded, "There is no reason to believe it was ever overt," his surmise is flawed. For one thing, although the above opinion was his own, he depended for basic information upon *Alger, A Biography Without A Hero* (Macy-Masius, 1928), by Herbert R. Mayes. In an article by Bill Henderson in *Publishers Weekly* (April 23, 1973), Mayes admitted that his book, a hoax which for forty-five years was accepted as reliable, "was undertaken with malice aforethought—a takeoff on the debunking biographies that were quite popular in the '20s."

Secondly, Tebbel took no notice of the fact that at the Newsboys' Lodging House there was present a Mrs. O'Connor, who continuously worked beside her husband as housemother. In a *New York Times* (February 26, 1964) review, Harrison E. Salisbury commented that Tebbel "contents himself with paperback Freudianism to explain one of the most revealing strands of the American dream."

In 1971, Dr. Richard M. Huber, a historian and educator (now Executive Director of Continuing Education at Hunter College), wrote *The American Idea of Success* (McGraw-Hill), a superb, multidisciplinary analysis of the work ethic. In this voluminous book, the author traced the lives and thoughts of numerous arbiters of success, from Benjamin Franklin to Dale Carnegie, devoting only 8 of 560 pages to Alger. He referred in a single paragraph to the Brewster incident, commenting, "Horatio Alger, Jr., without very much of a doubt, was a homosexual."

Disregarding the wealth of information Huber's work offered—

not to mention the years it took him to assemble it—the press pounced upon the Brewster lines, often mentioning little about the hefty volume's merits. *Newsweek* (February 7, 1972) used the homosexuality comment to lead into their report; the *Washington Star* (January 22, 1972) headlined a two-column feature "Was Horatio Alger Gay?"; and the *Detroit Free Press* (January 23, 1972) under a three-column headline declared "Horatio Alger Called a Homosexual." However, it should be noted, the *New York Times Book Review* (April 23, 1972) commented on Huber's "fact-freighted style" and "early expositors of the American Dream," Alger and the rest.

A lesser-known facet of Alger's talents was his ability as a classical scholar and linguist (Latin, Greek, French, and Italian), and as such he was sought as a tutor to children of prominent New York families. Social historian and best-selling author Stephen Birmingham noted this in two of his books, *Our Crowd* (Harper & Row, 1967) and *The Grandees* (Harper & Row, 1971). In *Our Crowd* Alger became tutor to the five sons of banker Joseph Seligman. Birmingham described Alger as "a timid, sweet-tempered little man who, in his non-teaching hours, practiced his ballet steps." Later, in *The Grandees* when Alger tutored future United States Supreme Court Justice Benjamin Cardozo to prepare him in 1884 for entrance exams to Columbia University, Birmingham described Alger as "flutily effeminate, with mincing ways and a fondness for practicing ballet positions in his spare time."

Stephen Birmingham told me he got this information from the late author and editor, Geoffrey T. Hellman, a descendant of Joseph Seligman. Such vignettes, Hellman explained to Birmingham, were reminiscences handed down through generations of family members.

Years ago I discussed Alger's mannerisms with United States Senator and former New York Governor Herbert H. Lehman and the retired diplomat Lewis Einstein. They both knew Alger in 1888, when they were about ten years old, and recalled him as being completely masculine in every way. But Einstein verified another point Hellman recalled to Birmingham: Alger was a natural-born fall guy for his students' pranks and practical jokes.

Perhaps it should be noted here that, aided by Alger's tutoring, Cardozo at age fourteen passed the Columbia entrance exams with a near perfect score. He was, however, required to wait until he reached fifteen to enter the university.

Newsman Leslie McFarlane, who under the stock pen name Franklin W. Dixon wrote a number of *Hardy Boys* stories for the Stratemeyer Syndicate, recalled in his biography *Ghost of The Hardy Boys* (Methuen/Two Continents, 1976) his onetime addiction to Alger's stories. Without heaping additional coal on the flames, he noted: "Maybe he was an unfrocked pastor . . . but in view of his parsonage background perhaps one can have sympathy for the distress he probably suffered in a society intolerant of any deviation from the hearty he-man mystique with its manly stench of beer, cigars, and honest sweat . . . Years ago he gave me hours of pleasure. More than that, a liking for books . . . Do I owe him anything? Yes, indeed I do."

The most damaging account was the one presented by Edwin P. Hoyt in *Horatio's Boys* (Chilton, 1974). Its cover, claiming that this was "The only tells-it-all biography" of Alger, went on to say in rather explicit terms that "Horatio Alger was *not* the American ideal personified. He was a slave to pederastic desires that even the most promiscuous followers of the American ideal still condemn as morally unacceptable . . . And the little boys he later idealized in his fiction were once the objects of his own homosexual persuasions." The Hoyt book's jacket copy declared: "Had he lived today, Alger might have been a charter member of the Gay Liberation movement." I do not know who wrote this dust jacket copy. An advertisement for the book announced: "Fully documented for the first time, here is the story of Rev. Alger's lifelong attempt to redeem himself from sin."

Of the book's 263 pages, Alger's Brewster days are mostly covered in six pages that comprise Chapter One. Much of the balance—although occasionally headed with such double-entendre titles as *The Unchangeable Alger, Lion Among the Juveniles,* and *The Brewster Affair*—is primarily plot summaries of Alger stories, fleshed out with biographical background for which Hoyt frequently depended upon other sources.

In a lengthy article on Alger in *American Opinion* (November, 1977), Medford Evans commented: "The absurdity of the 'charter member' libel of the dead is apparent. Whatever he did was not openly promoting homosexuality . . ."

One spin-off of Hoyt's book—listing it as the source—is Alger's inclusion in *Homosexuality: A History* (Meridian, 1979), by Vern L. Bullough. In one of the two brief entries about Alger, the author writes:

"Even such American folk heroes as Horatio Alger, Jr., were homosexual; his asexual boy heroes who gained success through living virtuous lives were perhaps his own sublimated way of expressing his homoerotic affection."

Michigan State University's Distinguished Professor of English, Pulitzer prize-winning biographer Russel Nye, discussed Hoyt's book with me when it first appeared. Then, in a letter dated January 11, 1975, he wrote: "You may remember my problem—reviewing Hoyt's *Horatio's Boys* for *Resources in American Literary Studies,* a rather prestigious and quite valuable literary journal. I decided it would be best not to review it at all—it clearly is not a 'literary source'—and so suggested to the editors, who have withdrawn it from consideration."

The knowledgeable commentator on Alger's life and writing, Prof. John Seelye, of the University of North Carolina, neatly sums up some of my own feelings in these opinions in *American Quarterly* (Winter, 1965): "Alger's character . . . contained certain unreconciled contradictions: despite his apparent mildness, he was a complex man, a product of conflicting desires and forces." In his introduction to the Book Club of California edition of Alger's *The Young Miner* (1965) he said: "One of the greatest of Ben Franklin's apostles (in terms of circulation) was a drab, shy, unsuccessful preacher named Horatio Alger, Jr. [who] turned to the full-time pursuit of what can only be called moral journalism . . . for periodicals whose eminent respectability qualified them for parlors and playrooms." And in the *New York Times Book Review* (March 25, 1973): "When he was fired because of suspected homosexuality, he spent the rest of his life writing for children . . . If Alger had indeed been an active homosexual, he would have been as a fox among chickens, but the very fact of his presence in the [Newsboys' Lodging House] for so many years suggests that, whatever his inclinations, he restrained them. Instead, proximity bred perceptiveness—Alger knew what boys wanted from a book better than most children's writers, then and now."

It is intriguing to note that—to this day—prominently displayed within the church in Brewster is a bronze plaque inscribed with the name of Horatio Alger, Jr., along with other clergymen who, before and after him, served that parish. If the accusations of 1866 did, indeed, cause him to depart in disgrace, would the congregation have thus commemorated his stay in their community?

Horatio Alger

THE SECOND SECRET; OR, ALWAYS A HAPPY ENDING

The same delightful innocence S. N. Behrman appreciated in Horatio Alger's juvenile books is present in the novels he wrote for adults, most of them written prior to his success as a children's writer. "Eventually, Alger would become one of the best-known authors of boys' books the world had ever known," wrote Quentin Reynolds, "but [during the mid-nineteenth century] he was determined to make his name with more 'serious' fiction."

Despite a clue first offered in 1918 by Frank M. O'Brien in his book *The Story of The Sun* (new edition, Greenwood Press, 1968), nine of these works—for a variety of reasons—remained mysteriously undiscovered until they were unearthed by the Alger scholar Stanley Pachon in the early 1950s. In the *Dime Novel Roundup* (September, 1973), he revealed that *Hugo, the Deformed, Madeline, the Temptress, The Secret Drawer, The Cooper's Ward, Herbert Selden, Manson, the Miser, The Gipsy Nurse, The Mad Heiress,* and *The Discarded Son* were serialized in *The Sun* between 1857 and 1860, during the years Alger attended the Cambridge Divinity School.

These were Alger's earliest novels, although he was already contributing short stories to a number of periodicals. The author's byline was printed over only four of them, while the first, *Hugo the Deformed*, appeared—for no apparent reason—under the pen name Charles F. Preston, with which Alger signed a number of short stories. Others were attributed to "By the Author of [preceding titles]."

The Cooper's Ward was twice rewritten by Alger to be reissued by Loring as bound volumes. In 1866 it was published, again anonymously, as *Timothy Crump's Ward.* This book is the most desired of the numerous Algers sought by collectors and institutions alike. In 1875 he again revised the story for a younger audience as *Jack's Ward.*

The Adult Novels

The two adult novels you are about to enjoy are truly vintage Alger. Read them for fun! *A Fancy of Hers* now appears for the first time as a bound volume under this title. In 1877 Alger was able to persuade Loring, whose top money-maker he had become, to print the story, but the publisher feared the possible consternation it might cause young fans who were then eagerly awaiting the already advertised *Wait and Hope* and Alger's forthcoming *Pacific Series.* Thus, he insisted that the novel, then titled *The New Schoolma'am; or, A Summer in North Sparta,* be issued anonymously in a small edition. It was not promoted as were Alger's juveniles and, probably to Loring's relief, was unnoticed and soon forgotten.

It was not, however, forgotten by its author and—eternally driven to create a significant reputation as a serious novelist—time and again he returned to it, altering names and places and updating the language and manners of his characters. Years later, with Loring retired and Alger now the star contributor to Frank A. Munsey's *Argosy,* he possessed sufficient clout to convince this publisher to print the revised work under his own name. Thus, it appeared in the March, 1892 issue of another of his employer's periodicals, *Munsey's Magazine.*

The story, featured as "The strange experiment of a New York girl—A village romance, and a series of sketches of village types—A novel complete in this issue," contained every bit of Alger's winning style and dialogue. Readers were invited to follow the adventures of Mabel Frost Fairfax, an enchanting, wealthy debutante, as she forsakes the social whirl and, incognito, seeks meaningful employment as a schoolteacher in the hamlet of Granville, New Hampshire. The scenes, situations, and repartee are genuine, delicious Alger and—especially regarding the trials of the financially depressed Congregational minister Theophilus Wilson and his family—contain generous autobiographical dollops of Alger's own childhood, with recollections of hardships and indignities suffered by his own father, The Rev. Horatio Alger, Sr.

A Fancy of Hers is brimful of the excitement and perpetual motion of Alger's more familiar works, plus Mabel's romance with Allan Thorpe, a poor but talented young artist who was "broad shouldered, wore a brown beard and had a pleasant, manly face lighted up by clear and expressive eyes."

The Disagreeable Woman, originally published by G. W. Dillingham in 1895, is a choice example of Alger's New York narratives, making it a marvelously balanced companion piece to the rusticity (S. N. Behrman suggested the word "verdancy") of *A Fancy of Hers.*

Dillingham had, a year earlier, asked Alger to do a book for him. They were friends since the days Dillingham worked for Loring. Later he joined G. W. Carleton—another Alger publisher—and took over ownership of that firm when Carleton retired. As Alger was under contract to Munsey for serialized juveniles and to Porter & Coates for hardcover editions, he offered—and Dillingham accepted—this recently completed adult novel. It was Munsey who, ever concerned about confusion it could cause among his youthful subscribers, insisted that an entirely new pseudonym be used. Hence the advent of Julian Starr, the name under which this story appeared. In happy anticipation, Alger wrote to a friend: "My small book will probably be published in June, in a dainty 75¢ form."

Soon after publication, a review in *Munsey's Magazine*—recommending it as "good, easy reading for a summer's day"—revealed that "Julian Starr is said to be the nom de plume of an author who is widely known in another literary field." For years this volume has remained one of the most elusive Alger treasures. There exist only the Library of Congress registration copy and one other, which was auctioned in 1975 at New York's Swann Gallery for $475 and ultimately cost its present owner $550. It would be a bargain at double that price!*

Readers familiar with Alger's unique style will readily identify him as the true author of *The Disagreeable Woman.* As described in my revised Alger bibliography *The Road to Success* (Wayside Press, 1971; now incorporated as a part of the 1978 Arco reissue of *Horatio Alger; or, The American Hero Era*), the residents of Mrs. Gray's rooming house on Waverly Place—where the action takes place—will be well known to Alger readers. Situations are familiar, with only the young Alger hero absent. Some of the author's favorite New York settings—the elegant Fifth Avenue Hotel at Madison Square, an early location of Macy's on Fourteenth Street, Delmonico's, the Brevoort House, and

**Twenty years ago, Alger novels could be picked from nickel-and-dime sidewalk stalls in front of bookshops. Today they are rare books, priced accordingly. Later reprints still cost about two to ten dollars, but first editions are something else. Three years ago a West Coast dealer sold* Bertha's Christmas Vision—*Alger's first book—for $350, and* Ragged Dick *for $750. In the 1978–1979 edition of* Book Collector's Handbook of Values *(Putnam), compiler Van Allen Bradley lists the worth of forty-three Alger first editions, including* Timothy Crump's Ward, *$2,000–$2,500;* Robert Coverdale's Struggle, *$500;* The Western Boy, *$200–$300;* Dan, the Detective, *$200–$250 (I know a couple of collectors ready to pay $400-plus for this one); and* The Five Hundred Dollar Check, *$250–$300. Some are marked as low as $30, but, for first editions in reasonably sound condition, $50 is closer to the average current price.*

others—are visited. One boarder even discusses "the hermit who lived in one of the cottages on the rocks near Central Park." This, of course, could be none other than Noah Outbank, the aged recluse known to readers of another Alger favorite, *Tom Tracy.*

The story's narrator, Dr. Fenwick, "who, after practicing for a year in a Jersey village had come to New York in quest of a metropolitan practice and reputation," bears a certain kinship to Nick Carraway, through whom F. Scott Fitzgerald a generation later told *The Great Gatsby.* Fenwick depicts Mrs. Gray's Wednesday evening soirees, at which Horton's ice cream was served, her "fair table [and] very social and entertaining family of boarders . . . from literateurs to dry goods clerks, school teachers, actors and broken down professionals." These include Prof. Poppendorf, who talks like a vaudeville Dutchman and "in consideration of his national tastes . . . was always supplied with a schooner of that liquid which is dear to the Teutonic heart," and Ruth Canby, "the young woman from Macy's" who, coming from Connecticut, where "she was raised among cabbages and turnips . . . had a fresh country face and complexion."

The center of attraction and mystery, of course, is the inscrutable Disagreeable Woman, who is aloof, secretive, and frequently sharp-tongued.

"To me," Fenwick remarked to a table neighbor, "she seems like an advocate of Woman's Rights."

But when he tells us that a "rare smile lighted up her features and made her positively attractive, in spite of her name," we know that she is definitely one of the right people; an odd sort of Alger *heroine* who, at a brisk pace, will lead us to another happy ending.

Ralph D. Gardner

A FANCY OF HERS

A FANCY OF HERS

CHAPTER ONE

The stage rumbled along the main street of Granville, and drew up in front of the only hotel of which the village could boast. The driver descended from his throne, and coming round to the side opened the door and addressed the only passenger remaining within.

"Where do you want to go, miss?"

A girl's face looked out inquiringly. "Is this the hotel?" she asked.

"Yes, miss."

"I will get out here," she said quietly.

There were a few loungers on the piazza, which extended along the whole front of the building. As she descended with a light and springy step, disregarding the proffered aid of the driver, they eyed her curiously.

"Who is she, Abner?" asked Timothy Varnum of the driver, as the stranger entered the house.

"I reckon she's the new school teacher," said Abner; "I heard Squire Hadley say she was expected today."

"Where does she come from?"

"York State, somewhere. I don't justly know where."

"Looks like a city gal."

"Mebbe, though I don't think it would pay a city gal to come to Granville to teach."

Unconscious of the curiosity which her appearance had excited, the girl entered the open entry and paused. A middle-aged woman, evidently the landlady of the inn, speedily made her appearance.

"Good afternoon, miss," she said. "Shall I show you to a room?"

"Thank you," said the stranger gratefully. "I shall be very glad if you will. The ride has been warm and dusty. My trunks are on the stage——"

"All right, miss, I'll have them sent up. If you'll follow me upstairs, I'll give you a room."

She led the way into a front room, very plainly furnished, but with a pleasant view of the village from the windows. "I think you will find everything you require," she said, preparing to go. "Supper will be ready in half an hour, but you can have it later if you wish."

"I shall be ready, thank you."

Left alone, the stranger sank into a wooden rocking chair, and gazed thoughtfully from the window.

"Well, I have taken the decisive step," she said to herself. "It may be a mad freak, but I must not draw back now. Instead of going to Newport or to Europe, I have deliberately agreed to teach the grammar school in this out-of-the way country place. I am wholly unknown here, and it is hardly likely that any of my friends will find me out. For the first time in my life I shall make myself useful—perhaps. Or will my experiment end in failure? That is a question which time alone can solve."

She rose, and removing her traveling wraps, prepared for the table.

The newcomer's two trunks were being removed from the stage when Mrs. Slocum passed, on her way to the store. Being naturally of a watchful and observant turn of mind, this worthy old lady made it her business to find out all that was going on in the village.

"Whose trunks are them, Abner?" she asked, in a voice high pitched even to shrillness.

"They belong to the young lady that's stoppin' in the hotel. She came in on the stage."

"Who's she?"

"I don't know any more'n you do," said Abner, who knew Mrs. Slocum's failing, and was not anxious to gratify it.

"There's her name on a card," said the old lady triumphantly, pointing to one of the trunks. "I hain't got my glasses with me. Just read it off, will you?"

Probably Abner had a little curiosity of his own. At all events he complied with the old lady's request, and read aloud:

"Miss Mabel Frost,
Granville, N. H."

"You don't say!" ejaculated Mrs. Slocum, in a tone of interest. "Why, it's the new school teacher! What sort of a looking woman is she?"

"I didn't notice her, partic'lar. She looked quite like a lady."

"Are both them trunks hern?"

"Yes, ma'am."

"What on airth does she want with two trunks?" said Mrs. Slocum, disapprovingly. "Must be fond of dress. I hope she ain't goin' to larn our gals to put on finery."

"Mebbe she's got her books in one of 'em," suggested Abner.

"A whole trunkful of books! Land sakes! You must be crazy. Nobody but a minister would want so many books as that. An' it's a clear waste for the parson to buy so many as he does. If he didn't spend so much money that way, his wife could dress a little more decent. Why, the man's got at least two or three hundred books already, and yet he's always wantin' to buy more."

"I guess his wife wouldn't want the trunks for her clothes," suggested Abner.

"You are right," said Mrs. Slocum, nodding. "I declare I'm sick and tired of that old bombazine she's worn to church the last three years. A stranger might think we stinted the minister."

"Precisely, Mrs. Slocum," said a voice behind her. "That's my opinion."

"Oh, Dr. Titus, is that you?" said the old lady, turning.

"What is left of me. I've been making calls all the afternoon, and I'm used up. So you think we are stinting the minister?"

"No, I don't," said Mrs. Slocum, indignantly. "I think we pay him handsome. Five hundred dollars a year and a donation party is more'n some of us get."

"Deliver me from the donation party!" said the doctor hastily. "I look upon that as one of the minister's trials."

"I s'pose you will have your joke, doctor," said Mrs. Slocum, not very well pleased. "I tell you a donation party is a great help where there's a family."

"Perhaps it is; but I am glad it isn't the fashion to help doctors in that way."

Dr. Titus was a free-spoken man, and always had been. His practice was only moderately lucrative but it was well known that he possessed a competency, and could live comfortably if all his patients deserted him; so no one took offense when he expressed heretical notions. He had a hearty sympathy for Mr. Wilson, the Congregational minister, who offended some of his parishioners by an outward aspect of poverty in spite of his munificient salary of five hundred dollars a year.

"The doctor's got queer notions," muttered Mrs. Slocum. "If he talks that way, mebbe the minister will get discontented. But as I say to Deacon Slocum, there's more to be had, and younger men, too. I sometimes think the minister's outlived his usefulness here. A young man might kinder stir up the people more, and make 'em feel more convicted of sin. But I must go and tell the folks about the new school teacher. I'd like to see what sort she is."

Mrs. Slocum's curiosity was gratified. On her way back from the store she saw Miss Frost sitting at the open window of her chamber in the hotel.

"Looks as if she might be proud," muttered the old lady. "Fond of dress, too. I don't believe she'll do for Granville."

Although Mrs. Slocum was in a hurry to get home she could not resist the temptation to call at Squire Hadley's and let him know that the school teacher had arrived. Squire Benjamin Hadley was the chairman of the School Committee. Either of the two Granville ministers would have been better fitted for the office, but the Methodists were unwilling to elect the Congregational minister, and the Methodist minister was opposed by members of the other parish. So Squire Hadley was appointed as the compromise candidate, although he was a man who would probably have found it extremely difficult to pass the most lenient examination himself. He had left school at twelve years of age, and circumstances had prevented his repairing the defects of early instruction. There were times when he was troubled by a secret sense of incompetence—notably when he was called upon to examine teachers. He had managed to meet this emergency rather cleverly, as he thought, having persuaded Mr. Wilson to draw up for him a series of questions in the different branches, together with the correct answers. With this assistance he was able to acquit himself creditably.

"Can't stay a minute, Squire," said Mrs. Slocum, standing on the broad, flat door stone. "I thought I'd just stop an' tell ye the school teacher has come."

"Where is she?" asked the Squire, in a tone of interest.

"She put up at the hotel. I was there jest now, and saw her two trunks. Rather high toned for a school teacher, I think. We don't need two trunks for *our* clothes, Mrs. Hadley."

"Young people are terrible extravagant nowadays," said Mrs. Hadley, a tall woman, with a thin, hatchet-like face, and a sharp nose. "It wasn't so when I was young."

"That's a good while ago, Lucretia," said the Squire, jokingly.

"You're older than I am," said the lady tartly. "It don't become you to sneer at my age."

"I didn't mean anything, Lucretia," said her husband in an apologetic tone.

"Did you see the woman, Mrs. Slocum?" asked Mrs. Hadley, condescending to let the matter drop.

"I jest saw her looking out of the window," said Mrs. Slocum. "Looks like a vain, conceited sort."

"Very likely she is. Mr. Hadley engaged her without knowin' anythin' about her."

"You know, Lucretia, she was highly recommended by Mary Bridgman in the letter I received from her," the Squire mildly protested.

"Mary Bridgman, indeed!" his wife retorted with scorn. "What does she know of who's fit to teach school?"

"Well, we must give her a fair show. I'll call round to the hotel after tea, and see her."

"It's her place to call here, I should say," said the Squire's wife, influenced by a desire to see and judge the stranger for herself.

"I will tell her to call here tomorrow morning to be examined," said the Squire.

"What hour do you think you'll app'int?" asked Mrs. Slocum, with a vague idea of being present on that occasion.

The Squire fathomed her design, and answered diplomatically, "I shall have to find out when it'll be most convenient for Miss Frost."

"Her convenience, indeed!" ejaculated his wife. "I should say that the School Committee's convenience was more important than hers. Like as not she knows more about dress than she does about what you've engaged her to teach."

"Where is she going to board?" asked Mrs. Slocum, with unabated interest in the important topic of discussion.

"I can't tell yet."

"I s'pose she'd like to live in style at the hotel, so she can show off her dresses."

"It would take all her wages to pay for board there," said the Squire.

"Mebbe I might take her," said Mrs. Slocum. "I could give her the back room over the shed."

"I will mention it to her, Mrs. Slocum," said the Squire diplomatically, and Mrs. Slocum hurried home.

"You don't really intend to recommend Mrs. Slocum's as a boarding place, Benjamin?" interrogated his wife. "I don't think much of the teacher you've hired, but she'd roast to death in that stived up back room. Besides, Mrs. Slocum is the worst cook in town. Her bread is abominable, and I don't wonder her folks are always ailing."

"Don't be uneasy about that, Lucretia," said the Squire. "If Miss Frost goes to Mrs. Slocum's to board, it'll have to be on somebody else's recommendation."

The new school teacher was sitting at the window in her room, supper being over, when the landlady came up to inform her that Squire Hadley had called to see her.

"He is the chairman of the School Committee, isn't he?" asked the stranger.

"Yes, miss."

"Then will you be kind enough to tell him that I will be down directly?" Squire Hadley was sitting in a rocking chair in the stiff hotel parlor, when Miss Frost entered, and said composedly, "Mr. Hadley, I believe?"

A Fancy of Hers

She exhibited more self possession than might have been expected of one in her position, in the presence of official importance. There was not the slightest trace of nervousness in her manner, though she was aware that the portly person before her was to examine into her qualifications for the post she sought.

"I apprehend," said Squire Hadley, in a tone of dignity which he always put on when he addressed teachers, "I apprehend that you are Miss Mabel Frost."

"You are quite right, sir. I apprehend," she added, with a slight smile, "that you are the chairman of the School Committee."

"You apprehend correctly, Miss Frost. It affords me great pleasure to welcome you to Granville."

"You are very kind," said Mabel Frost demurely.

"It is a responsible office—ahem!—that of instructor of youth," said the Squire, with labored gravity.

"I hope I appreciate it."

"Have you ever—ahem!—taught before?"

"This will be my first school."

"This—ahem! is against you, but I trust you may succeed."

"I trust so, sir."

"You will have to pass an examination in the studies you are to teach—before ME," said the Squire.

"I hope you may find me competent," said Mabel modestly.

"I hope so, Miss Frost; my examination will be searching. I feel it is my duty to the town to be very strict."

"Would you like to examine me now, Mr. Hadley?"

"No," said the Squire hastily, "no, no—I haven't my papers with me. I will trouble you to come to my house tomorrow morning, at nine o'clock, if convenient."

"Certainly, sir. May I ask where your house is?"

"My boy shall call for you in the morning."

"Thank you."

Mabel spoke as if this terminated the colloquy, but Squire Hadley had something more to say.

"I think we have said nothing about your wages, Miss Frost," he remarked.

"You can pay me whatever is usual," said Mabel, with apparent indifference.

"We have usually paid seven dollars a week."

"That will be quite satisfactory, sir."

Soon after Squire Hadley had left the hotel Mabel Frost went slowly up to her room.

"So I am to earn seven dollars a week," she said to herself. "This is wealth indeed!"

CHAPTER TWO

It is time to explain that the new school teacher's name was not Mabel Frost, but Mabel Frost Fairfax, and that she had sought a situation at Granville not from necessity but from choice—indeed from something very much like a whim. Hers was a decidedly curious case. She had all the advantages of wealth. She had youth, beauty, and refinement. She had the entrée to the magic inner circle of metropolitan society. And yet there was in her an ever present sense of something lacking. She had grown weary of the slavery of fashion. Young as she was, she had begun to know its hollowness, its utter insufficiency as the object of existence. She sought some truer interest in life. She had failed to secure happiness, she reasoned, because thus far she had lived only for herself. Why should she not live, in part at least, for others? Why not take her share of the world's work? She was an orphan, and had almost no family ties. The experiment that she contemplated might be an original and unconventional one, but she determined to try it.

But what could she do?

It was natural, perhaps, that she should think of teaching. She had been fortunate enough to graduate at a school where the useful as well as the ornamental received its share of attention, and her natural gifts, as well as studious habits, had given her the first place among her schoolmates.

The suggestion that the opportunity she sought might be found in Granville came from the Mary Bridgman to whom Squire Hadley referred. Mary was a dressmaker, born and reared in Granville, who had come to New York to establish herself there in her line of business. Mabel Fairfax had for years been one of her customers, and—as sometimes happens with society girls and their dressmakers—had made her a confidante. And so it happened that Mary was the first person to whom Miss Fairfax told her resolution to do something useful.

"But tell me," she added, "what shall I do? You are practical. You know me well. What am I fit for?"

"I hardly know what to say, Miss Fairfax," said the dressmaker. "Your training would interfere with many things you are capable of doing. I can do but one thing."

"And that you do well."

"I think I do," said Mary, with no false modesty. "I have found my path in life. It would be too humble for you."

"Not too humble. I don't think I have any pride of that kind; but I never could tolerate the needle. I haven't the patience, I suppose."

"Would you like teaching?"

"I have thought of that. That is what I am, perhaps, best fitted for; but I don't know how to go about it."

"Would you be willing to go into the country?"

"I should prefer it. I wish to go somewhere where I am not known."

"Then it might do," said Mary, musingly.

"What might do?"

"Let me tell you. I was born away up in the northern part of New Hampshire, in a small country town, with no particular attractions except that it lies not far from the mountains. It has never had more than a very few summer visitors. Only yesterday I had a letter from Granville, and they mentioned that the committee was looking out for a teacher for the grammar school, which was to begin in two weeks."

"The very thing," said Mabel quickly. "Do you think I could obtain the place?"

"I don't think any one has been engaged. I will write if you wish me to, and see what can be done."

"I wish you would," said Mabel promptly.

"Do you think, Miss Fairfax, you could be content to pass the summer in such a place, working hard, and perhaps without appreciation?"

"I should, at all events, be at work; I should feel, for the first time in my life, that I was of use to somebody."

"There is no doubt of that. You would find a good deal to be done; too much, perhaps."

"Better too much than too little."

"If that is your feeling I will write at once. Have you any directions to give me?"

"Say as little as possible about me. I wish to be judged on my own merits."

"Shall I give your name?"

"Only in part. Let me be Mabel Frost."

Thus was the way opened for Mabel's appearance in Granville. Mary Bridgman's recommendation proved effectual. "She was educated here; she knows what we want," said Squire Hadley; and he authorized the engagement.

When the matter was decided, a practical difficulty arose. Though Mabel had an abundant wardrobe, she had little that was suited for the school mistress of Granville.

"If you were to wear your last season's dresses—those you took to Newport," said Mary Bridgman, "you would frighten everybody at Granville. There would be no end of gossip."

"No doubt you are right," said Mabel. "I put myself in your hands. Make me half a dozen dresses such as you think I ought to have. There is only a week, but you can hire extra help."

The dresses were ready in time. They were plain for the heiress, but there was still reason to think that Miss Frost would be better dressed than any of her predecessors in office, partly because they were cut in the style of the day, and partly because Mabel had a graceful figure, which all styles became. Though Mary Bridgman, who knew Granville and its inhabitants, had some misgivings, it never occurred to Mabel that she might be considered overdressed, and the two trunks, which led Mrs. Slocum to pronounce her a "vain, conceited sort," really seemed to her very moderate.

At half past eight in the morning after Miss Frost's arrival in Granville Ben Hadley called at the hotel and inquired for the new school teacher.

"I guess you mean Miss Frost," said the landlord.

"I don't know what her name is," said Ben. "Dad wants her to come round and be examined."

Ben was a stout boy, with large capacities for mischief. He was bright enough, if he could only make up his mind to study, but appeared to consider time spent over his books as practically wasted. Physically and in temperament he resembled his father more than his mother, and this was fortunate. Mrs. Hadley was thin lipped and acid, with a large measure of selfishness and meanness. Her husband was pompous, and overestimated his own importance, but his wife's faults were foreign to his nature. He was liked by most of his neighbors; and Ben, in his turn, in spite of his mischievous tendencies, was a popular boy. In one respect he was unlike his father. He was thoroughly democratic, and never put on airs.

Ben surveyed Miss Frost, whom he saw for the first time, with approval, not unmingled with surprise. She was not the average type of teacher. Ben rather expected to meet an elderly female, tall and willowy in form, and wearing long ringlets. Such had been Miss Jerusha Colebrook, who had wielded the ferule the year before.

"Are you the school teacher?" asked Ben dubiously, as they left the hotel.

Mabel smiled. "I suppose," said she, "that depends on whether I pass the examination."

"I guess you'll pass," said Ben.

"What makes you think so?" asked Mabel, amused.

"You look as if you know a lot," answered Ben bluntly.

"I hope appearances won't prove deceptive," said Mabel. "Are you to be one of my scholars?"

"Yes," replied Ben.

"You look bright and quick."

"Do I?" said Ben. "You can't always tell by looks," he added, parodying her own words.

"Don't you like to study?" Mabel inquired.

"Well, I don't hanker after it. The fact is," said Ben in a burst of confidence, "I'm a pretty hard case."

"You say so because you are modest."

"No, I don't; the last teacher said so. Why, she couldn't do nothing with me."

"You begin to alarm me," said Mabel. "Are there many hard cases among the scholars?"

"I'm about the worst," said Ben candidly.

"I'm glad to hear that."

"Why?" asked Ben, puzzled.

"Because," said Mabel, "I don't expect to have any trouble with you."

"You don't?" said Ben, surprised.

"No, I like your face. You may be mischievous, but I am sure you are not bad."

Ben was rather pleased with the compliment. Boy as he was, he was not insensible to the grace and beauty of the new teacher, and he felt a thrill of pleasure at words which would scarcely have affected him if they had proceeded from Jerusha Colebrook.

"Do you feel interested in study?" Mabel continued.

"Not much," Ben admitted.

"You don't want to grow up ignorant, do you?"

"Of course I want to know something," said Ben.

"If you improve your time you may some time be chairman of the School Committee, like your father."

Ben chuckled. "That don't take much larnin'," he said.

"Doesn't it? I should think it would require a good scholar."

Ben laughed again. "Perhaps you think my father knows a good deal?" he said interrogatively.

Ben seemed on the brink of a dangerous confidence, and Mabel felt embarrassed.

"Certainly," said she.

"He don't," said Ben. "Don't you ever tell, and I'll tell you something. He got the minister to write out the questions he asks the teachers."

"I suppose the minister was more used to it," said Mabel, feeling obliged to proffer some explanation.

"That ain't it," said Ben. "Dad never went to school after he was twelve. I could cipher him out of his boots, and he ain't much on spelling, either. The other day he spelled straight s-t-r-a-t-e."

"You mustn't tell me all this," said Mabel gravely. "Your father wouldn't like it."

"You won't tell him?" said Ben apprehensively, for he knew that his father would resent these indiscreet revelations.

"No, certainly not. When does school commence, Ben?"

"Tomorrow morning. I say, Miss Frost, I hope you'll give a good long recess."

"How long have you generally had?"

"Well, Miss Colebrook only gave us five minutes. She was a regular old poke, and got along so slow that she cut us short on recess to make it up."

"How long do you think you ought to have?" asked Mabel.

"Half an hour'd be about right," said Ben.

"Don't you think an hour would be better?" asked Mabel, smiling.

"May be that would be too long," Ben admitted.

"So I think. On the other hand I consider five minutes too short. I will consult your father about that."

"Here's our house," said Ben suddenly. "Dad's inside waiting for you."

Squire Hadley received Mabel with an impressive air of official dignity. He felt his importance on such occasions. "I am glad to see you, Miss Frost," he said.

"Are there any other teachers to be examined?" asked Mabel, finding herself alone.

"The others have all been examined. We held a general examination a week ago. You need not feel nervous, Miss Frost. I shall give you plenty of time."

"You are very considerate, Squire Hadley," said Mabel.

"I will first examine you in arithmetic. Arithmetic," here the Squire cleared his throat, "is, as you are aware, the science of numbers. We regard it as of primary—yes, *primary* importance."

"It is certainly very important."

"I will—ahem—ask you a few questions, and then give you some sums to cipher out. What is a fraction, Miss Frost?"

Squire Hadley leaned back in his chair, and fixed his eyes prudently on that page of the arithmetic which contained the answer to the question he had asked. Mabel answered correctly.

"You have the correct idea," said the Squire patronizingly, "though you ain't quite got the phraseology of the book."

"Definitions vary in different arithmetics," said Mabel.

"I suppose they do," said the Squire, to whom this was news. To him arithmetic was arithmetic, and it had never occurred to him that there was more than one way of expressing the same thing.

Slender as was his own stock of scholarship, Squire Hadley knew enough to perceive, before going very far into the textbook, that the new school teacher was well up in rudimentary mathematics. When he came to geography, however, he made an awkward discovery. He had lost the list of questions which the minister had prepared for him. Search was unavailing, and the Squire was flustered.

"I have lost my list of questions in geography," he said, hesitatingly.

"You might think of a few questions to ask me," suggested Mabel.

"So I can," said the Squire, who felt that he must keep up appearances. "Where is China?"

"In Asia," answered Mabel, rather astonished at the simple character of the question.

"Quite right," said the Squire, in a tone which seemed to indicate surprise that his question had been correctly answered. "Where is the Lake of Gibraltar?"

"I suppose you mean the Straits of Gibraltar?"

"To be sure," said the Squire rather uneasily. "I was—ahem! thinking of another question."

Mabel answered correctly.

"Where is the River Amazon?"

"In South America."

Squire Hadley had an impression that the Amazon was not in South America, but he was too uncertain to question the correctness of Mabel's answer.

"Where is the city of New York situated?" he asked.

Mabel answered.

"And now," said the Squire, with the air of one who was asking a poser, "can you tell me where Lake Erie is located?"

Even this did not overtask the knowledge of the applicant.

"Which is farther north, New York or Boston?" next asked the erudite Squire.

"Boston," said Mabel.

"Very well," said the Squire approvingly. "I see you are well up in geography. I am quite satisfied that you are competent to teach our grammar school. I will write you a certificate accordingly."

This the Squire did; and Mabel felt that she was one step nearer the responsible office which she had elected to fill.

"School will begin tomorrow at nine," said the Squire. "I will call round and go to school with you, and introduce you to the scholars. I'll have to see about a boarding place for you."

"Thank you," said Mabel, "but I won't trouble you to do that. I will stay at the hotel for a week, till I am a little better acquainted. During that time I may hear of some place that I shall like."

Squire Hadley was surprised at this display of independence.

"I apprehend," he objected, "that you will find the price at the hotel too high for you. We only pay seven dollars a week, and you would have to pay all of that for board."

"It will be for only one week, Squire Hadley," said Mabel, "and I should prefer it."

"Just as you say," said the Squire, not altogether satisfied. "You will be the first teacher that ever boarded at the hotel. You wouldn't have to pay more'n three dollars at a private house."

"Of course that is a consideration," said Mabel guardedly.

As she left the Squire's house and emerged into the road she heard steps behind her. Turning, she saw Ben Hadley.

"I say, Miss Frost, was you examined in geography?" he asked.

"Yes, Ben."

"Did dad ask you questions off a paper?"

"No; he couldn't find the paper."

"I thought so," said Ben grinning.

"Do you know what became of it?" asked Mabel, with sudden suspicion.

"Maybe I do and maybe I don't," answered Ben, non-committally. "What sort of questions did dad ask you?"

"Wait till school opens," answered Mabel, smiling; "I will ask you some of them there."

"Did he really and truly examine you in geography out of his own head?" asked Ben.

"Yes, Ben; he didn't even open a book."

"Good for dad!" said Ben. "I didn't think he could do it."

"It is quite possible that your father knows more than you give him credit for," said Mabel.

"Guess he must have remembered some of the questions," thought Ben.

In the course of the day the list of geographical questions found its way back to Squire Hadley's desk.

"Strange I overlooked it," he said.

Perhaps Ben might have given him some information on the subject.

CHAPTER THREE

The Granville schoolhouse was not far from the center of the village. It was wholly without architectural ornament. The people of Granville, it must be admitted, were severely practical, and were not willing to spend a dollar in the interest of beauty. Their money was the result of hard labor, and frugality was not to be wondered at. In a commercial community architecture receives more attention.

The schoolhouse was two stories in height, and contained two schools. The primary school, for children under eight, was kept in the lower room. The grammar school, for more advanced scholars, which Mabel Frost had undertaken to teach, occupied the upper portion of the building.

As Mabel approached the schoolhouse, escorted by Squire Hadley, she noticed, a few rods in advance, a tall, slender woman, with long ringlets falling over a pair of narrow shoulders.

"That lady is your colleague, Miss Frost," said the Squire.

"My colleague?" repeated Mabel, in a tone of inquiry.

"Yes; she keeps the primary school."

"Indeed! Then there is another school besides mine!"

"To be sure. Miss Clarissa Bassett teaches the youngest children."

"Is she—does she live here?"

"Yes; she has taught the same school for fifteen years. All your scholars began with her."

"Then she isn't a very young lady?"

"Clarissa," replied the Squire, with that familiarity which is common in small villages, "must be thirty-five, though she only owns up to twenty-five," added he, chuckling. "Might spile her matrimonial prospects if she confessed her real age."

"Fifteen years a teacher!" said Mabel enthusiastically. "Miss Bassett ought to feel proud of such a term of service. How much good she has done!"

"Well, I dunno," said Squire Hadley, whose practical mind conceived of no other motive for teaching than the emolument to be derived from it. "Clarissa wanted to teach the grammar school—the same that you're a goin' to teach; but we didn't think she was qualified to teach advanced scholars."

"And you preferred me before a teacher of fifteen years' experience!" said Mabel, with unaffected humility. "I am afraid, Squire Hadley, you will find that you have made a mistake."

"You are a better scholar than Clarissa, Miss Frost. She knows enough to teach the little ones, but——"

"She has fifteen years' experience, and I have none," interrupted Mabel.

"You wouldn't be willing to change schools with her?" suggested the Squire, with mild satire.

"Yes, I would," said Mabel promptly.

"She don't get but six dollars a week—a dollar less than you."

"I don't care for that."

"The deestrict wouldn't be satisfied," said the Squire, in a decided tone. Mabel was an enigma to him. "They wouldn't be willing to have Clarissa teach the older pupils," he repeated.

By this time they had reached the schoolhouse. Some twenty pupils were outside, most of them Mabel's future scholars. Miss Bassett had paused in the entry, and awaited the arrival of Squire Hadley and her fellow teacher. She had a thin face, and that prim expression regarded as the typical characteristic of an old maid. It had been her lot to see the companions of her early days sail off, one after another, on the matrimonial sea, while she had been left neglected on the shore. She had even seen some of her pupils—mere chits, as she called them—marry, while their teacher, with all her experience of life, was unappropriated.

"Miss Frost," said Squire Hadley, with a wave of his hand toward Clarissa, "let me make you acquainted with Miss Bassett, who has kept our primary school for fifteen years with general acceptance and success."

"You ought to be regarded as a public benefactor, Miss Bassett," said Mabel cordially.

"I was *very* young when I commenced teaching," said Miss Bassett, rather uneasy at the allusion to her term of service.

"I am a beginner," said Mabel. "I shall be glad to have an experienced teacher so near to me, to whom I can refer in cases of difficulty."

Clarissa, who had been prejudiced against Mabel, because, although so much younger, she had been placed over the other's head, was flattered by this acknowledgment of inferiority.

"I shall be very glad to give you any help in my power, Miss Frost," she said. "You will excuse me now; I must go in and look after my young pupils."

Miss Frost followed Squire Hadley upstairs to the scene of her future labors.

The room itself was an average country schoolroom. It had accommodations for about fifty scholars. The desks, on the boys' side, were covered with ink spots of all shapes and sizes, and further decorated with an extensive series of jackknife carvings. Mabel's neatness was rather offended by these things, which she took in in her first general survey. It was not much like any school that she had ever attended; but a private academy for girls differs essentially from a country schoolroom for both sexes.

"I see most of the scholars are here," said Squire Hadley.

Mabel looked around the room. Between forty and fifty scholars, varying in age from eight to sixteen, were seated at the desks. At her entrance, they had taken seats previously selected. For the most part she liked their appearance. Several looked mischievous, but even they were bright eyed and good natured. All eyes were fixed upon her. She felt that she was being critically weighed in the balance by these country boys and girls.

"I wonder what are their impressions of me," she thought. "I wonder if they suspect my inexperience!"

The children did not pronounce judgment at once. Their first impressions were favorable. They were surprised by the sight of so attractive a teacher. Mabel did not look like a school mistress—certainly not like Clarissa Bassett. Ben Hadley had told his friends something of her, and had even spoken in enthusiastic terms.

"She's as pretty as a picture," he had told them. "I bet she won't be an old maid."

The boys, in particular, had their curiosity excited to see her and judge for themselves. Now that they saw her they fully coincided with Ben's opinion. They were still regarding their new teacher when Squire Hadley broke the silence.

"Scholars," he said, clearing his throat, and assuming the attitude of an orator, "I have great pleasure in introducing to you your new teacher, Miss Frost. I have examined Miss Frost," he proceeded, in a tone of importance, "and I find that she is thoroughly competent to lead you in the flowery paths of learning." (This was a figure on which the Squire rather prided himself.) "She comes to us highly recommended, and I have no doubt you will all like her. As chairman of the committee," (here the Squire's breast expanded with official pride), "I have tried to obtain for you teachers of the highest talent, without regard to expense." (Had the Squire forgotten that Mabel was to receive only seven dollars a week?) "I trust—the town trusts—that you will appreciate what we are doin' for you. We want you to attend to your studies, and work hard to secure the blessin's of a good education, which is the birthright of every citizen. I will now leave you in charge of your teacher, and I hope you will study to please her."

The Squire sat down, and drawing an ample red handkerchief from his pocket wiped his brow with some complacency. He felt that his speech was a success. He had not stumbled, as he sometimes did. He felt that he had done credit to his position.

"Now I must go down to Miss Bassett's school," he added, rising to go. "I must say a few words to her scholars. Miss Frost, I wish you success in your—ahem!—very responsible task."

"Thank you, sir."

The ample form of the Squire vanished through the closing door, and Mabel was left face to face with her new responsibilities. For a moment she was nervous. She knew little of the routine of a country school, and felt like a civilian who without a particle of military training finds himself suddenly in command of a regiment.

"I wonder what I ought to do first," she thought, in some perplexity. She would have consulted Squire Hadley on this point had she not hesitated to reveal her utter lack of experience.

While glancing about the room in an undecided way she detected Ben Hadley slyly preparing to insert a pin into the anatomy of the boy next him. This gave her an idea.

"Ben Hadley, please come to the desk," she said quietly.

Ben started guiltily. He decided that the school teacher had seen him, and was about to call him to account. His face wore a half defiant look as he marched up to the desk, the observed of all observers. All the scholars were on the *qui vive* to learn the policy of the new administration. This summons seemed rather a bold move, for Ben was generally regarded as the head of the opposition. Not from malice, but from roguery, he gave successive teachers more trouble than any other scholar. Had the new school mistress found this out, and was she about to arraign the rebel as her first act of power? Such was Ben's suspicion, as, with his head erect, he marched up to the teacher's desk.

To his surprise Miss Frost met him with a friendly smile.

"Ben," said she pleasantly, "you are one of the oldest scholars, and the only one whom I know. Are you willing to help me organize the school?"

Ben was astonished. That such a proposal should be made to him, the arch rebel, was most unexpected.

"Guess she don't know me," he thought. But yet he felt flattered; evidently he was a person of some consequence in the eyes of the new teacher.

"I'll help you all I can, Miss Frost," he said heartily.

"Thank you, Ben, I felt sure you would," said Mabel, with quiet confidence. "I suppose the first thing will be to take the names of the scholars."

"Yes, Miss Frost; and then you sort 'em into classes."

"To be sure. How many classes are there generally?"

"Well, there are three classes in reading, and two in arithmetic, and two in geography."

"That is just the information I want. Now, Ben, I will ask you to go about with me, and tell me the names of the scholars."

But before entering upon this formality, Mabel, for the first time in her life, made a speech.

"Scholars," she said, "I am a stranger to you, but I hope you will come to regard me as your friend. I am here to help you acquire an education. I am sure you all wish to learn. There is a great satisfaction in knowledge, and it will help you, both boys and girls, to become useful men and women, and acquit yourselves creditably in any positions which you may be called upon to fill. I am not so well acquainted with the method of carrying on a country grammar school as most of my predecessors, having myself been educated in the city. I have, therefore, asked Ben Hadley to assist me in organizing the school, and preparing for work."

The scholars received the announcement with surprise. It presented Ben to them in a novel character. They waited with interest to see how he would acquit himself in his new office.

Ben accompanied Miss Frost from desk to desk, and greatly facilitated her task by his suggestions. At length the names of all the scholars were taken.

"Now I must arrange the classes," said Mabel, with increased confidence. "Have you any advice to give, Ben?"

"You'd better ask the first class to come up," suggested her young assistant. "Then you'll know exactly who belongs to it."

"That will be the best plan," said Mabel; and she followed his advice.

Ben left her side and took his place in the class. He scanned the class, and then said: "Miss Frost, there's one boy here who belongs in the second class."

At this revelation a boy standing next but one to Ben showed signs of perturbation.

"Who is it?" asked the teacher.

"John Cotton."

"Do you belong to this class, John?"

"I ought to; I know enough," said he sullenly.

"Today you will oblige me by taking your place in the second class. In a few days I can decide whether you are able to go with this class."

John retired, discontented, but hopeful.

"I shall be glad when any of you are fit for promotion," proceeded Mabel. "At first it will be best for the classes to remain as they were during the last session."

So the organization continued. By noon the school was ready for work; lessons had been assigned in grammar, geography, and arithmetic, and the first class had read.

"I think we have done a good morning's work," said Miss Mabel Frost as the clock struck twelve. "I believe our afternoon session commences at one. I should like to have you all punctual."

In leaving the schoolroom to go to dinner, Mabel passed Ben Hadley. "You have been of great service to me, Ben," said she with a smile. "I really don't know how I should have got along without you."

Ben blushed with gratification. It was long since he had felt so proud and well pleased with himself.

"How do you like your new teacher, Ben?" asked his father at the dinner table.

"She's a trump, father," said Ben, warmly.

"Then you like her?" asked the Squire in some astonishment, for he understood perfectly well Ben's school reputation. Indeed, more than one teacher had come to him to complain of his son and heir's mischievous conduct, and he had had misgivings that Miss Frost would have occasion to do the same thing.

"Yes, I do," said Ben, emphatically. "She knows how to treat a feller."

"Then there was no disturbance?"

"Not a speck."

The Squire was greatly surprised.

"I helped organize the school," proceeded Ben proudly.

"YOU!" exclaimed the Squire, in small capitals.

"Certainly. Why shouldn't I?"

"I apprehend that you might need organizing yourself," said the Squire, smiling at what he considered a witty remark.

"Maybe I do, sometimes," said Ben, "but I like Miss Frost, and I mean to help her."

"I didn't see much in her," said Mrs. Hadley, opening her thin lips disapprovingly. "In my opinion she dresses too much for a teacher."

"I don't see why she shouldn't if she can afford it," said Ben, who had constituted himself Mabel's champion.

"She can't afford it on her wages," retorted his mother.

"I guess that's her lookout," said Ben, hitting the nail on the head.

"Ben's taken an uncommon fancy to the school mistress," said Squire Hadley, after Ben had returned to school.

"It won't last," said Mrs. Hadley, shaking her head. "He'll soon be up to his old tricks again, take my word for it. I don't believe she'll suit, either. A new broom sweeps clean. Just wait a while."

"If it does last—I mean Ben's fancy—it will be surprising," said the Squire. "He's been a thorn in the side of most of the teachers."

"It won't last," said Mrs. Hadley decidedly, and there the conversation dropped.

CHAPTER FOUR

Ben Hadley's conversion had indeed been sudden, and, as in most similar cases, he found some difficulty in staying converted. While his pride was flattered by the confidence reposed in him by Miss Frost, there were times when his old mischievous propensities almost overcame him. On the third day, as John Cotton was passing Ben's desk, the latter suddenly thrust out his foot into the passageway between the desks, and John tumbled over it, breaking his slate.

"What's the matter?" asked Mabel, looking up from the book from which she was hearing another class.

"Ben Hadley tripped me up," said John, rubbing his shins, and looking ruefully at his broken slate.

"Did you, Ben?" asked Mabel.

Ben was already sorry and ashamed, as he would not have been under any other teacher. With all his faults he was a boy of truth, and he answered "Yes," rather sheepishly.

"You should be careful not to keep your feet in the aisle," said Miss Frost quietly. "I suppose you'll be willing to buy John a new slate."

"Yes," said Ben promptly, glad to have the matter end thus.

"I need a slate now," grumbled John.

"I'll lend you mine," said Ben at once, "and buy you a better one than I broke."

Mabel quite understood that the accident was "done on purpose." She did not want to humiliate Ben, but rather to keep him on his good behavior. So she was as friendly and confidential as ever, and Ben preserved his self respect. He kept his promise, and bought John the most expensive slate he could find in the village store.

Mabel very soon found herself mistress of the situation. Experience goes for a good deal, but it does not always bring with it the power of managing boys and girls. Mabel seemed to possess this instinctively. Before the week was out, all was running smoothly in her department, a little to the disappointment of Miss Clarissa Bassett, who felt that the school should have been hers.

Mabel still boarded at the hotel. She was quietly on the lookout for a more desirable boarding place.

Among her scholars was a little girl of nine, whose cheap dress indicated poverty, but who possessed a natural refinement, which in her was more marked than in any other pupil. Mabel inquired into her circumstances, and learned that her father had been an officer in the army, who had died soon after his marriage. All that he left to his widow was a small cottage, and a pension of twenty dollars a month to which his services entitled her. On this small sum, and a little additional earned by sewing, Mrs. Kent supported her family, which, besides Rose, included a boy two years younger, who was in Miss Bassett's school. One afternoon Mabel walked home with Rose, and introduced herself to Mrs. Kent. She found her a delicate and really refined woman, such as she imagined Rose would grow to be in time. Everything in the house was inexpensive, but there were traces of good taste about the little establishment.

"I am glad to see you, Miss Frost," said Mrs. Kent, with quiet cordiality. "I have heard of you continually from Rose, who is your enthusiastic admirer."

"Rose and I are excellent friends," said Mabel, smiling kindly on the little girl. "She never gives me any trouble."

"I have never heard of any complaints from any of her teachers.

One thing that I have heard surprises me, Miss Frost. You have wonderfully changed Ben Hadley, who had been the torment of previous teachers."

Mabel smiled. "I like Ben," she said. "From the first I saw that he had many good points. He was merely mischievous."

"Merely?" repeated Mrs. Kent smiling.

"Mischief may give a good deal of trouble, but the spirit that leads to it may be turned into another channel. This I think I have done with Ben. I find him very bright when he exerts his abilities."

"You understand managing boys, I can see clearly. Yet I hear that this is your first school."

"I have never entered a country school till I commenced teaching here."

"Your success is wonderful."

"Don't compliment me prematurely, Mrs. Kent. Failure may yet be in store for me."

"I think not."

"And I hope not."

"You are living at the hotel, I believe?"

"Only temporarily. I am looking for a pleasant boarding place."

"Mrs. Breck might be willing to take you. She has boarded several teachers before."

Mabel had met Mrs. Breck. She had the reputation of being a good housekeeper, but withal she was a virago, and her husband a long suffering victim of domestic tyranny. She was a thin little woman, with a shrewish face, who was seldom known to speak well of anybody.

"I don't think I should enjoy boarding with Mrs. Breck," said Mabel. "I'm sure I should like your house much better."

"You don't know how plainly we live," said Mrs. Kent. "I should like very much to have you here, but my table doesn't compare with Mrs. Breck's."

"Let me make you a business proposition, Mrs. Kent," said Mabel, straightforwardly. "I don't pretend to be indifferent to a good table, and I know the small amount usually paid for a teacher's board would not justify you in changing your style of living. I propose, if you will be kind enough to receive me, to pay you ten dollars a week as my share of the expenses."

"Ten dollars!" ejaculated Mrs. Kent in utter amazement. "Why, Mrs. Breck only charges three."

"But I would rather pay the difference and board with you."

"Excuse me, Miss Frost, but how can you? Your salary as teacher must be less than that."

"I see that I must tell you a secret, Mrs. Kent. I depend on your not making it public. I am quite able to live without touching a penny of my salary."

"I am glad of that," said Mrs. Kent, "but it seems so extortionate, my accepting ten dollars a week!"

"Then don't let any one know how much I pay you. It will imperil my secret if you do. Am I to consider myself accepted?"

"I shall be *very* glad of your company, Miss Frost, and I know Rose will be delighted."

"Will you come here, really and truly, Miss Frost?" asked Rose eagerly.

"Since your mother is willing, Rose."

Rose clapped her hands in delight, and showed clearly how acceptable the arrangement was to her.

Mabel's choice of a boarding place excited general surprise in Granville. "I wish the school teacher joy of her boarding place," said Mrs. Breck, tossing her head. "Why, Widder Kent has meat only once or twice a week; and once, when I called about supper time, I noticed what she had on the table. There wasn't nothing but cold bread and butter, a little apple sauce, and tea. It'll be something of a change from the hotel."

"She lives better now," said Mrs. Cotton. (This was several days after Mabel had become an inmate of Mrs. Kent's house.) "I called yesterday on purpose to see what she had for supper, and what do you think? She had cold meat, eggs, preserves, warm bread, and two kinds of pies."

"Then all I can say is, that the woman will be ruined before the summer's out," said Mrs. Breck, solemnly. "What the school teacher pays her won't begin to pay for keepin' such a table as that. It's more'n I provide, myself, and I don't think my table is beat by many in Granville. Mrs. Kent's a fool to pamper a common school teacher in any such way."

"You're right, Mrs. Breck; but, poor woman, I suppose she has to. That Miss Frost probably forces her to it. I declare it's very inconsiderate, for she must know the widow's circumstances."

"It's more than inconsiderate—it's sinful," said Mrs. Breck, solemnly.

"Mrs. Kent can't be very prudent to go to such expense," said the other party to this important discussion.

"Miss Frost flatters Rose, and gets around the mother in that way. She's a very artful young woman, in my opinion. The way she pets that Hadley boy, they say, is positively shameful."

"So I think. She wants to keep on the right side of the School Committee, so as to get the school another term."

"Of course. That's clear enough," chimed in Mrs. Breck. "I should like to know, for my part, a little more about the girl. Nobody seems to know who she is or where she came from."

"Squire Hadley engaged her on Mary Bridgman's recommendation, I hear."

Mrs. Breck sniffed. "Mary Bridgman may know how to cut dresses," she remarked, "though it's my opinion there's plenty better; but it's a new thing to engage teachers on dressmakers' recommendations. Besides, there's Clarissa Bassett, one of our own folks, wanted the school, and it's given to a stranger."

Miss Bassett boarded with Mrs. Breck, and this may have warped the good lady's judgment.

"I don't know as I'm in favor of Clarissa," said Mrs. Cotton, "but there's others, no doubt, who would be glad to take it."

"As for Miss Frost, I don't see how she is able to dress so well. That gown she wears to school must have cost two weeks' salary, and I've seen her with two other dresses."

"And all new?"

"Yes, they don't look as if they had had much wear."

"Perhaps she's seen better days, and has saved them dresses from the wreck."

"But you forget that they look new."

"Well, I give it up. It's clear she puts all her money on her back. A pretty example for our girls!"

Such were the comments of the mothers. Among the children, on the other hand, Mabel grew more and more popular. She succeeded in inspiring an interest in study such as had not been known before. She offered to teach a class in French and one in Latin, though it entailed extra labor.

"She knows an awful lot, father," said Ben Hadley.

"She was my selection," said the Squire complacently. "You

predicted she would make a failure of it, Mrs. Hadley. The fact is we have never had a better teacher."

"The school term isn't closed," said Mrs. Hadley oracularly. "Appearances are deceitful."

It is rather singular that Mabel was favorably regarded by the fathers, while the mothers, to a man, were against her. There is something wrong in this sentence, but let it stand.

CHAPTER FIVE

In an old fashioned house a little east of the village lived the Rev. Theophilus Wilson, pastor of the Congregational Church in Granville. The house was considerably out of repair, and badly needed painting. It belonged to Squire Hadley, of whom the minister hired it, together with an acre of land adjoining, for seventy-five dollars a year. An expenditure of one or two hundred dollars would have improved its appearance and made it a little more habitable, and the Squire, who was not a mean man, would have consented to this outlay but for the strenuous opposition of his wife.

"It's good enough for the minister," she said. "Ministers shouldn't be too particular about their earthly dwellings. I believe in ministers being unworldly, for my part."

"The house does look rather bad," said the Squire. "Mrs. Wilson says the roof leaks, too."

"A few drops won't hurt all the furniture she's got," said Mrs. Hadley contemptuously.

Mrs. Hadley was rather inconsistent. She regarded the minister's poor furniture and his wife's worn dresses with scornful superiority; yet, had either complained, she would have charged them with worldliness.

"One coat of paint won't cost much," said the Squire, watching his wife's countenance for signs of approval or the opposite.

"It will do no good," said she positively. "It won't make the house any warmer, and will only conduce to the vanity of the minister and his wife."

"I never thought either of them vain," expostulated her husband.

"You only look to the surface," said his wife, in a tone of calm superiority. "I go deeper. You think, because Mrs. Wilson can't afford to dress well, that she has no vanity. I can read her better. If she had the means she'd cut a dash, you may depend upon it."

"There's one thing I can't understand, Lucretia," said her husband. "Why are things worldly in them that are not in us?"

"I don't know what you mean."

"You like to dress well, and I like my house to look neat. Why doesn't that show a worldly spirit in us?"

"Because you are not a minister nor I a minister's wife."

"What difference does that make?"

"You are very dull this morning, Mr. Hadley," said his wife scornfully.

"Perhaps I may be, but still I should like an explanation."

"Ministers should set their hearts on things above."

"Shouldn't we?"

"Not in the same way. They should be humble and not self seeking. They should set a good example to the parish. Does Mr. Wilson pay his rent regular?" she asked, suddenly changing the subject.

"Tolerable."

"Isn't he in arrears?"

"I can't tell exactly without looking at the books," said the Squire evasively.

"I understand; you don't want to tell me. I dare say he is owing you half a year's rent."

This was quite true, but Squire Hadley neither confirmed nor denied it. He could quite understand that Mr. Wilson, with a wife and three children, found it hard to keep even with the world on his scanty stipend, and he did not feel like pressing him.

"I think it shameful for a minister not to pay his debts," said Mrs. Hadley, in an acid tone.

"Suppose he can't, my dear."

"Don't dear me. I am out of patience with you," said the lady sharply.

"Why?"

"You needn't ask. You encourage the minister in his shiftless course."

"Suppose I had three children, and all our clothing and household expenses had to be paid out of five hundred a year."

"If you was a minister you ought to do it."

"A minister can't make a dollar go any farther than other people."

"He can give up luxuries and vanities."

"Our minister indulges in very few of those," said the Squire, shrugging his shoulders.

"I don't know about that. I saw Sarah Wilson in the store the other day buying some granulated sugar, when brown is cheaper and would do equally as well."

"I believe we use granulated sugar, Lucretia," said Squire Hadley, his eyes twinkling.

"You're not a minister."

"And I shouldn't want to be if the sinners are to get all the good things of this life, and the saints have to take up with the poorest."

"Call yourself a sinner if you like, but don't call me one, Mr. Hadley," said his wife with some asperity.

"Ain't you a sinner?"

"We are all sinners, if it comes to that, but I consider myself as good as most people. How much rent did you say the minister was owing you?"

"I didn't say," said the Squire shrewdly.

"Keep it a secret if you please. All I say is that it's a duty you owe your family to collect what is honestly due you. I would do it if I were a man."

"I think you would, Lucretia. However, to please you, I'll attend to it within a week."

"I am glad you're getting sensible. You allow your good nature to run away with you."

"I am glad you allow me one good quality, Lucretia," said her husband with an attempt at humor.

Mrs. Hadley did not fail to inquire of her husband, a few days afterward, if the rent had been collected, and heard with satisfaction that it had been paid up to the current month.

"I told you he would pay it if you pressed him," she said triumphantly.

Her husband smiled. He thought it best not to relate the circumstances under which it had been paid. He had called at the minister's study the day after the conversation above detailed, and after a few remarks on indifferent topics said:

"By the way, Mr. Wilson, in regard to the rent——"

"I regret being so much in arrears, Squire Hadley," said the minister uncomfortably; "but really it is a very perplexing problem to make my salary cover the necessary expenses of my family. I hope in a few weeks to be able to pay something."

"Don't trouble yourself, my dear sir," said the Squire genially. "You must find it difficult, I am sure. I find, by my books, that you are owing me six months' rent."

"I am afraid it is as much as that," said Mr. Wilson, sighing.

"And I am going to help you to pay it."

The minister looked at his guest in surprise. Squire Hadley took out his pocket book, and drew therefrom four ten dollar bills.

"Mr. Wilson," said he, "I make you a present of this, and now, perhaps, you will be able to pay me the rent due—thirty-seven dollars and a half, I think the exact amount is."

"My good friend," said the minister, almost overcome, "how can I thank you for this generosity?"

"By paying me my rent," said the Squire smiling. "I am very particular to have that paid promptly. If you will furnish me with writing materials I will write you a receipt. Now, Mr. Wilson," he added, as he rose to go, "I am going to ask you a favor."

"Only mention it, my friend."

"Let this little transaction be a secret between us."

"It is hard to promise that; I should like to speak to others of your goodness. If I say nothing about it, it will seem ungrateful."

"If you do mention it, you will get me into hot water."

"How is that?" inquired the minister, in some perplexity.

"The fact is my wife is very frugal, and just a leetle stingy. She can't help it, you understand. Her father was pretty close fisted. She wouldn't approve of my giving away so much money, and might remonstrate."

"Yes, I understand," said the minister, who knew, as all the village did, that Mrs. Hadley was quite as close fisted as her lamented father.

"So we had better say nothing about it."

"I can tell my wife?"

"Yes, you may tell her, for it may relieve her from anxiety. Of course she won't mention it."

"You are a firm friend, Squire Hadley," said Mr. Wilson, grasping the hand of his parishioner cordially. "You are one of those who do good by stealth, and blush to find it fame."

"No, I ain't," said Squire Hadley bluntly; "I should be perfectly willing to have all my good deeds known if it was not for Mrs. Hadley.

Dozens of bullies rued the day they took a swing at one of Alger's heroes. Besides being honest, enterprising, and respectful, these robust lads were handy with their fists.

The Western Boy *soon was reissued as* Tom the Bootblack, *the title under which it became one of the author's best-loved books. Here street-wise Tom, a lad "of enterprising disposition," tells a customer he is "ready to adopt a rich father."*

In Brave and Bold, *as in a number of Alger's adventure tales, the hero is shipwrecked, to be rescued by a passing vessel.*

At the hands of wicked conspirators, the Alger hero was slugged, chloroformed, shanghaied, and occasionally thrown into an abandoned well.

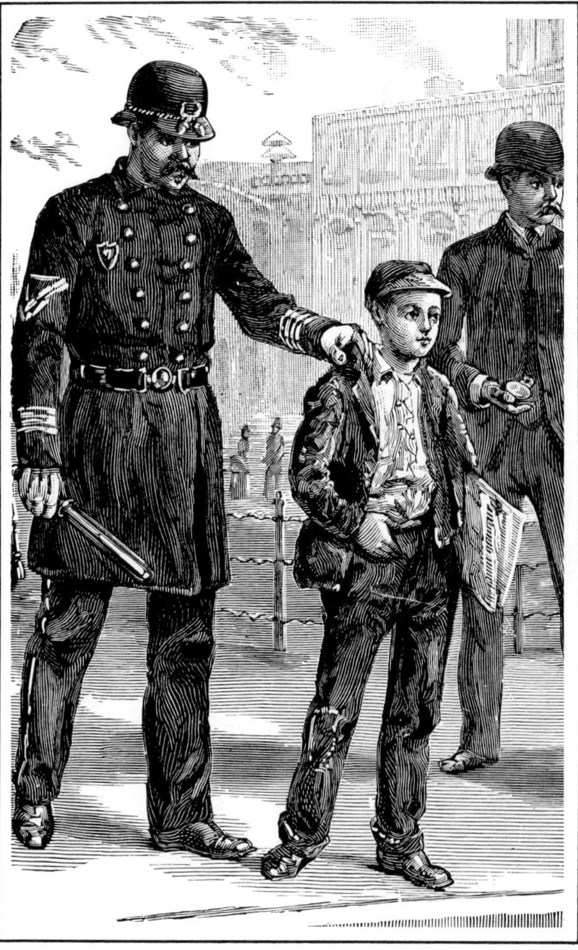

Like many other young heroes, Tom Tracy was framed and falsely arrested. Of course, the tables were turned in short order.

Ragged Dick dove into the East River to save a life. A heroic rescue often was the hero's first step up the ladder of success.

In Brave and Bold, *Robert Rushton risked his life to flag down a train that was "speeding towards him at the rate of twenty-five miles an hour!"*

Frank Manton, in Silas Snobden's Office Boy, *returns a wallet he found.*

The grateful benefactor often invited the young hero to his Madison Avenue home. His "winsome, flirtatious" daughter found the visitor fascinating.

At the conclusion of Sink or Swim, *Harry Raymond returns in the nick of time to save the old homestead and thwart the villainous Squire Turner. "Foiled at all points," Alger wrote, "he dashed his hat angrily upon his head and rushed from the house in undignified haste."*

Many young heroes left the farm to seek their fortune. They lived clean, won fame and fortune, and returned in time to pay off the mortgage.

The First Parish Unitarian Church of Brewster, Massachusetts, where Alger served as minister from 1864 until 1866.

The Newsboys Lodging House on Fulton Street. Here many of the street boys, whose adventures Alger chronicled, boarded for six cents a night.

It was a Lodging House rule that all residents must wash before entering the dining room.

An engraved portrait of Horatio Alger, Jr., that was offered as an incentive to readers of The Argosy.

THE GOLDEN ARGOSY

Entered according to Act of Congress, in the year 1887, by FRANK A. MUNSEY, in the office of the Librarian of Congress, at Washington, D. C.

Vol. V.—No. 47. FRANK A. MUNSEY, PUBLISHER. 81 WARREN ST., NEW YORK. NEW YORK, SATURDAY, OCTOBER 22, 1887. TERMS $3.00 PER ANNUM IN ADVANCE. Whole No. 255.

WALTER GRIFFITH FELT A HEAVY HAND ON HIS SHOULDER, AND, LOOKING UP, HE SAW TO HIS DISMAY THAT HE WAS IN THE GRASP OF A POLICEMAN.

WALTER GRIFFITH;

OR,

THE ADVENTURES OF A YOUNG STREET SALESMAN.

By ARTHUR LEE PUTNAM,

Author of "Ned Newton," "Tom Tracy," "Number 91," etc., etc., etc.

CHAPTER I.

WALTER IN BROOKLYN.

A BOY of fifteen, with a healthy brown upon his face, walked down Fulton Street, in Brooklyn, with a small bundle of clothes tied up in a red silk handkerchief. He looked about him with a curious eye, for he had never before been in a city. He was very much impressed by the large and showy stores which line this—the chief business street of New York's sister city.

"I wonder if New York is any bigger than Brooklyn," he said, almost unconsciously giving utterance to the thought.

"Well, I should smile if it wasn't," responded another voice.

Turning his head, Walter Griffith's eyes fell upon a boy dressed in a blue uniform,

Cover of Golden Argosy. *It features* Walter Griffith *who, fresh from the country, is duped by a confidence man and gets in trouble with the law. This story is by-lined Arthur Lee Putnam, another of Alger's pen names.*

Volume VI. Number 6. Price 25 cts.—$3 a Year.

MUNSEY'S MAGAZINE

FOR MARCH, 1892.

PAGE

"Phædra," . . . . Frontispiece
From the Painting by Alexandre Cabanel.

Famous Artists and Their Work—III. Alexandre Cabanel, ... C. Stuart Johnson . . 635
With Reproductions of some of his most Celebrated Paintings.

Secrets, A Poem. . . . . S. S. Stinson . . . 641

The German Student Duel, ... W. Thornton Parker, M.D. 642
The famous *Mensur* described by a former Member of one of the Student Corps—Illustrated.

The Reformed Church in New York, . . . R. H. Titherington . 650
An Outline of the Past and Present of the oldest Church Organization of the Metropolis—with Portraits and Illustrations.

Pierre's Story, ... Hinton McMillan . . 662

Emma Eames, ... Owen Hackett . . 666
A Critique of the celebrated young American Prima Donna, with Portraits of her in her leading characters.

Treasure Trove, A Short Story. . . . . William S. Lawrence . 673

The Chinese Quarter of New York, . . . Warren Taylor . . 678
Illustrated with sketches of the Metropolitan Chinatown and its Oriental inhabitants.

Paderewski, ... Morris Bacheller . . 683
With a Portrait of the famous Pianist.

The Maloney Conservatory, A Short Story. . . Tudor Jenks . . . 687

A Morning with the Pope, ... W. H. W. Campbell . 689
A Glimpse of the daily life of His Holiness Leo XIII, illustrated with views of the Vatican.

The Dawn of Love, A Poem, Illustrated. . . . Judson Newman Smith . 696

A Fancy of Hers, ... Horatio Alger, Jr. . 697
The strange Experiment of a New York Girl—a Village Romance, and a series of sketches of Village Types—A Novel Complete in this Issue.

Mrs. Raymond's Cousin, A Short Story. . . . Matthew White, Jr. . 745

Etchings, ... 752
JUST AS OF OLD—CHOATE'S FIRST FEE—A RONDEAU OF REMORSE—A CALIFORNIA PIONEER—A BOSTON WOOING—HENRY CLAY IN A TIGHT PLACE—A RETROSPECT—SEEING AND KNOWING.

Impressions by the Way, ... 754
THE FIRST MILESTONE—THE NEW FRENCH TARIFF LAW—IMMIGRATION AND DISEASE—SOUTH AMERICAN REPUBLICS.

FRANK A. MUNSEY & COMPANY, 155 EAST 23D STREET, NEW YORK

ALL MATTER IN MUNSEY'S MAGAZINE IS COMPLETE IN EACH ISSUE.

Cover of Munsey's Magazine *dated March, 1892, listing* A Fancy of Hers, *by Horatio Alger, Jr.*

The old Fifth Avenue Hotel, at Madison Square. Here many Alger heroes were invited to dine with fatherly benefactors, often to the disgust of the swaggering snob, who wondered what the humble bootblack was doing in the company of one of New York's social leaders. (Reprinted from 1866 New York Directory, *courtesy of Schocken Books.)*

Delmonico's, a favored dinner and after-theater meeting place in many of Alger's tales. The author himself was among the restaurant's regular patrons. (Courtesy of the New-York Historical Society. Reprinted from Old New York in Photographs, *published by Dover Publications, Inc.)*

Macy's, located during the 1890s at Sixth Avenue and Fourteenth Street. Here Miss Ruth Canby, whom we meet in the The Disagreeable Woman, *was employed. (Photo courtesy of R. H. Macy & Co., Inc. Reprinted from* Nation's Business.*)*

Strive and Succeed! The world's temptations flee
Be Brave and Bold! and Strong and Steady be!
Shift for yourself, and prosper then you must!
Win Fame and Fortune while you Try and Trust!

Horatio Alger Jr.

Feb. 22d 1890.

Alger occasionally inscribed books with this verse, constructed around the titles of six of his stories.

And that reminds me, I would willingly paint the house for you if she did not object."

"That is not of so much consequence; but the roof does leak badly, and troubles my wife a good deal."

"That ought to be fixed," said the Squire. "How shall I manage it?"

He reflected a moment, and his face brightened with a new idea.

"I'll tell you what, Mr. Wilson, we must use a little strategy. You shall see a carpenter, and have the roof repaired at your own expense."

Mr. Wilson's countenance fell. "I fear——" he commenced.

"But I will repay you whatever it costs. How will that do?"

"How kind you are, Squire Hadley!"

"It is only what I ought to do, and would have done before if I had thought how to manage it. As Mrs. Hadley will wonder how you raised the money, I will say you had a gift from a friend, and that I told you to repair the house at your own expense."

A few days later Mrs. Hadley came home in some excitement. "Mr. Hadley," said she, severely, "I find that the minister's house is being new shingled."

"Is it?" asked her husband indifferently.

"This is the way you waste your money, is it?"

"What have I to do with it? If Mr. Wilson chooses to shingle the house at his own expense, I am perfectly willing."

"Didn't you order it done?" inquired his wife, in amazement.

"Certainly not. The minister spoke of it when he paid the rent, and I told him he could do it at his own expense if he chose to."

"That's just what you ought to have said. But I don't understand where the minister finds the money, if he is so poor as you say he is."

"I understand that he has received a gift of money from a friend," said the diplomatic Squire.

"I didn't know he had any friend likely to give him money. Do you know who it is?"

"He didn't tell me, and I didn't inquire," answered the Squire, pluming himself on his strategy.

"Was it a large sum?"

"I don't think it was."

"I wish his friend had given him enough to pay for painting the house, too."

"Why? The house wouldn't be any warmer for painting," said the Squire slyly.

"It would look better."

"And so minister to his vanity."

"You seem to be very stupid this morning," said Mrs. Hadley, provoked.

"I am only repeating your own observations, my dear."

"If Mr. Wilson can afford to paint the house, I am in favor of his doing it; but I don't think you have any call to pay for it. The house will be better property if it is newly painted."

"Then don't you think I ought to do it, Lucretia?"

"No, I don't," said Mrs. Hadley sharply.

"I think myself," said the wily Squire, "considering the low rate at which the minister gets the house, he could afford to put on one coat of paint at his own expense. I have a great mind to hint it to him."

"You'd better do it, Mr. Hadley," said his wife approvingly.

"I will; but perhaps he won't look at it in the same light."

Within a week the painters were at work on the parsonage. The coat of paint improved its appearance very much. I suspect the bill was paid in the same way as the shingling; but this is a secret between the minister and Squire Hadley, whose strategy quite baffled his wife's penetration.

CHAPTER SIX

"Please, Miss Frost, the sewing society is going to meet at our house this afternoon, and mother wants you to come round after school, and stay to supper."

The speaker was Annie Peabody, daughter of Deacon Uriah Peabody, a man who lived in a groove, and judged all men according to his own experience of life, which was very limited. He was an austere, old fashioned Calvinist, who believed that at least nineteen-twentieths of his fellow men were elected to perdition. Mr. Wilson's theology was not stern enough to suit him. He characterized the minister's sermons as milk and water.

"What we want, parson, is strong meat," he more than once remarked to the minister. "You're always exhortin' men to do right. I don't take much stock in that kind of talk."

"What shall I preach then, Deacon Peabody?" asked the minister mildly.

"If I were a minister I'd stir up the sinners," said the deacon emphatically.

"How would you do it?"

"I'd describe the lake of fire, and the torments of the damned, an' let 'em understand what is prepared for 'em if they don't fear God and do his commandments."

The minister shuddered a little. He was a man of sensitive organization, upon whom these gloomy suggestions jarred unpleasantly. "I can't paint such lurid pictures, deacon," he answered; "nor do I feel that they would do any good. I don't want to paint our Maker as a cruel tyrant, but as a merciful and considerate Father."

"I'm afeared, parson, that you ain't sound in the doctrines. You know what the Scriptures say, 'Vengeance is mine; I will repay, saith the Lord.' "

"We also read, 'Like as a father pitieth his children, so the Lord pitieth them that fear him.' "

"But suppose they don't fear him," said the deacon triumphantly.

"I believe in the punishment of sin," returned Mr. Wilson. "We cannot err without incurring the penalty, but I believe God, in punishing the sinner, does not cease to love him. 'Whom he loveth he chasteneth:' or, as we have a right to say, he loves those that he chastens."

"I don't know about that," said the deacon. "I think that's twistin' Scripture to our own ends. How many do you think are goin' to be saved, Parson Wilson?"

"I cannot hazard a conjecture, deacon. Heaven forbid that I should seek to limit the goodness and mercy of God."

"Do you think a quarter will be saved?" persisted the deacon. "Of course I don't mean the heathen. There ain't no hope for any of them, unless they've been converted by the missionaries. I mean of them that's brought up under Christian institutions."

"A quarter? Most certainly. If I felt that three-quarters of the race were destined to be lost, my soul would be weighed down with grief."

"Well, for my part," said the deacon, "I've no idea that as many as a quarter will be saved. About one in twenty is full as high as I calc'late on."

"Good Heavens! Deacon Peabody, you can't be in earnest."

"Yes, I be. Why, Parson Wilson, look at the people as they are," (the deacon pronounced it air)—"ain't they steeped in folly and vice? Ain't they carnally minded? Ain't they livin' for this world without no thought of the other? Air they fit for the mansions of the blest? Tell me that."

The deacon's voice rose in a sort of crescendo, and he put the last question triumphantly.

"We are none of us fit for Heaven," replied the minister, "but we can rely on God's mercy. Your doctrine is simply horrible. If but one in twenty is to be saved, don't you feel anxious about your own soul.

"Of course I'm a poor, miserable sinner," said the deacon complacently; "but I'm a professin' Christian, and I have faith in Christ. I think I come within the promises."

"Suppose you were sure of your own salvation, doesn't the thought of the millions who are to perish ever give you anguish?"

"Of course I'm sorry for the poor, deluded sinners," said the deacon, who managed nevertheless to maintain a cheerful exterior; "but the peace of God remains in my soul, and I don't allow the folly of others to disturb me."

The minister shook his head.

"If I believed as you do, deacon," he said, "I could not close my eyes at night. I could not rejoice in the bright sunshine and glorious beauty of outward nature. I should put on sackcloth and ashes, and pour out my soul to God in earnest prayer that he would turn his soul from wrath."

"I don't feel like interferin' with God's arrangements. I've no doubt they're for the best."

"You think it best that all heathen and nineteen-twentieths of those that live in Christian countries should be damned?" asked the minister with some vehemence.

"If it's the Lord's will," said Deacon Peabody, in a sanctified tone, "I'm resigned to it."

Deacon Peabody should have lived at least fifty years earlier. He found few of his contemporaries to agree with him in his rigid notions. Most of the parish sympathized rather with the milder theology of Mr. Wilson. Had it been otherwise, had the deacon thought it possible to obtain a preacher in harmony with his own stern views, he would have headed a movement to get rid of the minister. As it was, he contented himself with protesting, in public and private, against what he regarded as pernicious and blinding error.

This has been a long digression, but the deacon was a prominent man in Granville, and interesting as the representative of a class numerous in Puritan days.

When Mabel entered the deacon's parlor, after school was over, she found some dozen ladies congregated, including the most prominent matrons of Granville. There were but two other young ladies besides Miss Frost. One of them was Miss Clarissa Bassett, the other a grown up daughter of the deacon—Miss Charity Peabody, who was noted for a lack of that virtue which had been given her as a designation. Mrs. Peabody, in strange contrast to her husband, had a heart overflowing with kindness, and was disposed to look on the best side of everybody.

"I am very glad to see you, Miss Frost," said Mrs. Peabody cordially, advancing to meet the school teacher. "I've meant to call, but I couldn't seem to get time. I suppose you know some of these ladies. I'll introduce you to such as you don't know."

So Mabel made the rounds and was generally introduced. Though the society was so unlike that in which she had been accustomed to mingle, she had a natural grace and tact which carried her through the ordeal easily and naturally. She finally found a seat next to Mrs. Priscilla Pulsifer, an old lady of an inquiring turn of mind, who was a new acquaintance, and promptly seized the opportunity to cross-examine Mabel, as she had long desired to do.

"You're the new school teacher, ain't you?"

"Yes, I am."

"How old be you?" asked the old lady, glaring at her through her glasses.

"Twenty-two," answered Mabel, resenting what she considered an impertinent question by a counter inquiry. "How old are you, Mrs. Pulsifer?

"Seventy-one; and I ain't ashamed on't, either," answered the old lady, bridling.

Mabel was already sorry for her question. "Age is not a thing to be ashamed of," she said. "You don't look so old as that."

"So folks say," said Mrs. Pulsifer, quite appeased, and resuming her inquiries: "You're from the city, ain't you?"

"Yes."

"Ever taught afore?"

"This is my first school."

"How do you like teachin'?"

"Better than I expected. I feel repaid for my labor by watching the progress of the scholars."

"How much wages do you get?" asked the old lady practically.

"Seven dollars a week."

"That's pooty good pay for a single gal," remarked Mrs. Pulsifer. "You don't have anybody dependent on you?"

"Do you mean a husband, Mrs. Pulsifer?" asked Mabel, her eyes sparkling with fun.

"I didn't know but you might have a mother, or brother an' sister, to support."

"No," said Mabel sadly, "I am alone in the world."

"Sho! I s'pose you calc'late on bein' married some time," said the old lady, with directness.

"Perhaps I may be," said Mabel, amused, "but I can't say I calculate on it."

"I guess you can get somebody to marry you," said the practical old lady. "You're good lookin', and are likely to please the men. Clarissa Bassett's tried hard, but somehow she don't make out."

Miss Bassett was sitting at the other end of the room, and, fortunately, was engaged in conversation with Mrs. Hayden, so that she did not hear this last remark.

"Thank you," said Mabel demurely. "You quite encourage me."

"I was twenty-five myself before I was married," continued Mrs. Pulsifer. "Not but what I had offers before. Maybe you've had a chance?" and the old lady scrutinized Mabel's countenance.

"Maybe I have," she answered, wanting to laugh.

"That's a pooty gown you have on," said Mrs. Pulsifer, her attention diverted by Mabel's dress. "Was it made in the city?"

"Yes."

"Looks like nice cloth," continued Mrs. Pulsifer, taking a fold between her thumb and finger.

"I think it is," answered Mabel.

"How much was it a yard?"

"I'm afraid I don't remember," Mabel replied.

The fact is, she had intrusted the purchase of her summer dresses to her dressmaker, who rendered her the bill in a lump. If there were any details she did not remember them.

"That's strange," said the old lady, staring. "I know the price of all the clothes I ever bought."

"You probably have a better memory than I," said Mabel, hoping by this compliment to turn the attack, but in vain.

"Haven't you any idee of the price?" asked the old lady.

"It may have been a dollar a yard."

"How many yards did you get?"

"I—am not sure."

"How much did you pay for that collar?"

"I am really sorry I can't tell you," said Mabel, who felt somewhat embarrassed.

"Perhaps you don't like to tell."

"I would tell you with pleasure, if I knew."

"'Pears to me you must be a poor manager not to keep more account of your expenses," said Mrs. Pulsifer.

"I am afraid I am," said Mabel.

"How many dresses did you bring with you, Miss Frost?"

The old lady's catechizing was getting annoying, but Mabel understood that she meant no offense and answered patiently, "Six."

"Did they all cost as much as this?"

"I should think so."

"I don't see how you can afford to spend so much on dress," said Mrs. Pulsifer, "considering you have only seven dollars a week salary."

"I shall try to be more prudent hereafter, Mrs. Pulsifer."

"You'd better. The men will be afraid to marry you if they think you're extravagant. I told my son Jotham, 'Jotham,' says I, 'don't you marry a woman that wants to put all her money on her back.' Says I, 'An extravagant wife is a curse to a man that wants to be forehanded.' "

"Did your son follow your advice?"

"Yes; he married a likely girl that makes all her own dresses. Jotham told me only last week that he didn't buy her but one dress all last year."

"You must be pleased with your daughter-in-law, Mrs. Pulsifer."

"Yes; she's pretty good as wives go nowadays, but I don't think she's a good cook."

"That is a pity."

"Can you cook, Miss Frost?"

"I don't know much about cooking."

"Sho! You'll want to know how when you're married."

"When I see any chance of marrying I mean to take lessons," said Mabel.

Just then, to Mabel's relief, supper was reported to be ready, and the members of the sewing society filed out with alacrity to the sitting room, where a long table was bountifully spread with hot biscuit, preserves, and several kinds of cake and pies. The mistress of the household, rather flushed by the heat of the kitchen, welcomed her guests, and requested them to take seats. Mabel took care not to sit in the neighborhood of Mrs. Pulsifer. The old lady's curiosity had come to be annoying, yet could not well be resented.

She congratulated herself on finding her next neighbor to be Mrs. Wilson, the minister's wife, a small woman, in a well worn silk, ten years old, which had been her only "company dress" during tht entire period. There was a look of patient anxiety on the good woman's face which had become habitual. She was sorely perplexed at all times to make both ends meet. Even now she was uncomfortable in mind from this very cause. During the morning Mr. Bennett, the butcher, had called at the parsonage, and urgently requested payment for his "little bill." It amounted to only twenty-five dollars, but the minister's stock of ready money was reduced to five dollars, and to pay this on account would have left him penniless. His candid statement of his pecuniary condition was not well received.

"I don't think people ought to buy meat if they can't pay for it," said the butcher bluntly.

"The parish is owing me more than the amount of your bill, Mr. Bennett," said the perplexed minister. "Just as soon as I can collect the money——"

"I need it now," said the butcher coarsely. "I have bills to pay, and I can't pay them unless my customers pay me."

"I wish I could pay you at once," said Mr. Wilson wistfully. "Would you take an order on the parish treasurer?"

"No; he's so slack it wouldn't do me any good. Can't you pay half today, Mr. Wilson?"

"I have but five dollars on hand, Mr. Bennett; I can't pay you the whole of that. I will divide it with you."

"Two dollars and a half! It would be only ten per cent of my bill."

He closed, however, by agreeing to take it; but grumbled as he did so.

"These things try me a good deal," said the minister, with a sigh, after the departure of his creditor. "I sometimes think I will leave the profession, and try to find some business that will pay me better."

"It would be hazardous to change now, Theophilus," said his wife. "You have no business training, and would be as likely to do worse as better."

"Perhaps you are right, my dear. I suppose we must worry along. Do you think we could economize any more than we do?"

"I don't see how we can. I've lain awake many a night thinking whether it would be possible, but I don't see how. We couldn't pinch our table any more without risking health."

"I am afraid you are right."

"Why not call on Mr. Ferry, the treasurer, and see if he cannot collect some more money for you?"

"I will do so; but I fear it will be of no use."

The minister was right. Mr. Ferry handed him two dollars.

"It is all I have been able to collect," he said. "Money is tight, Mr. Wilson, and everybody puts off paying."

This was what made Mrs. Wilson's face a shade more careworn than usual on this particular day. To add to her trouble, Mrs. Bennett, the wife of her husband's creditor, who was also a member of the sewing circle, had treated her with great coolness, and almost turned her back upon her. The minister's wife was sensitive, and she felt the slight. When, however, she found Mabel at her side she smiled pleasantly.

"I am glad to have a chance to thank you, Miss Frost, for the pains you have taken with my little Henry. He has never learned so fast with any teacher before. You must have a special talent for teaching."

"I am glad if you think so, Mrs. Wilson. I am a novice, you know. I have succeeded better than I anticipated."

"You have succeeded in winning the children's love. Henry is enthusiastic about you."

"I don't think I should be willing to teach unless I could win the good will of my scholars," said Mabel, earnestly. "With that, it is very pleasant to teach."

"I can quite understand your feelings. Before I married Mr. Wilson, I served an apprenticeship as a teacher. I believe I failed as a disciplinarian," she added, smiling faintly. "The committee thought I wasn't strict enough."

"I am not surprised," said Mabel. "You look too kind to be strict."

"I believe I was too indulgent; but I think I would rather err in that than in the opposite direction."

"I fancy," said Mabel, "that you must find your position as a minister's wife almost as difficult as keeping school."

"It certainly has its hard side," said Mrs. Wilson cautiously; for she did not venture to speak freely before so many of her husband's parishioners.

Just then Mrs. Bennett, the butcher's wife, who sat on the opposite side of the table, interrupted their conversation. She was a large, coarse looking woman, with a red face and a loud voice.

"Miss Frost," she said, in a tone of voice audible to all the guests, "I have a bone to pick with you."

Mabel arched her brows, and met the glance of Mrs. Bennett with quiet haughtiness.

"Indeed!" said she, coldly.

"Yes, indeed!" replied Mrs. Bennett, provoked by the cool indifference of the school teacher.

"Please explain," said Mabel quietly.

"You promoted two girls in my Flora's class, and let her stay where she was."

"I would have promoted her if she had been competent."

"Why ain't she competent?" Mrs. Bennett went on.

"Of course there can be only one answer to that question, Mrs. Bennett. She is not sufficiently advanced in her studies."

"She knows as much as Julia Fletcher or Mary Ferris, any day," retorted Mrs. Bennett.

"Suppose we defer our discussion till we leave the table," said Mabel, finding it difficult to conceal her disdain for her assailant's unmannerly exhibition.

Mrs. Bennett did not reply, but she remarked audibly to the woman who sat next to her; "The school teacher's rather uppish. 'Pears to me she's carryin' things with a high hand."

"You see a school teacher has her trials, Mrs. Wilson," said Mabel, turning to her neighbor with a rather faint smile.

"I feel for you," said the minister's wife sympathetically.

"Thank you, but don't suppose I mind it at all. I shall exercise my own discretion, subject only to the committee. I am wholly independent."

"I wish I could be," sighed Mrs. Wilson; "but no one can be less so than a minister's wife."

"Is your husband to be here this evening?" asked Mabel.

"He has a bad headache and was unable to come. I shall go home early, as I may be needed."

In fact, about half an hour later, Mrs. Wilson made an apology and took her leave.

"Mrs. Wilson is looking pale and careworn," said Mrs. Kent. "Don't you think so, Mrs. Hadley?"

"She hasn't much energy about her," replied the Squire's wife. "If she had, the minister would get along better."

"I think she's no sort of manager," said Mrs. Bennett. "She runs her husband into debt by her shiftless ways."

"I think you're mistaken," said Mrs. Pratt quietly. "I know her well, and I consider her an admirable manager. She makes a little go as far as she can, and as far as any one else could."

"I only know my husband can't get his bill paid," Mrs. Bennett went on. "He presented it this morning—twenty-five dollars—and only got two dollars and a half. Seems to me there must be poor management somewhere."

It would be unfair to the femininity of Granville to say that Mrs. Bennett was a fair specimen of it. Except Mrs. Hadley, there was not one who did not look disgusted at her coarseness and bad breeding.

"You must excuse me, Mrs. Bennett," said Mrs. Kent, "but I don't think that follows, by any means, from what you say."

"Then how do you explain it?" asked the butcher's wife.

"The trouble is that Mr. Wilson's salary is too small."

"He ought to live on five hundred dollars a year, I think," said Mrs. Hadley; "especially when he gets his rent so cheap."

"Is five hundred dollars actually the amount of his salary?" asked Mabel, amazed.

"Yes."

"How do you expect him to support his family on such an amount as that?" she exclaimed almost indignantly.

"It is very small, Miss Frost, "said Mrs. Pratt, "but I am afraid we couldn't pay much more. None of us are rich. Still I think something ought to be done to help Mr. Wilson. What do you say, ladies, to a donation visit?"

"It's just the thing," said Clarissa Bassett enthusiastically.

"It may be better than nothing," said Mrs. Kent; "but I am afraid donation visits don't amount to as much as we think they do."

The proposal, however, was generally approved, and before the meeting closed it was decided to give the minister a donation visit a fortnight later.

"Shall you be present, Miss Frost?" asked Mrs. Pratt.

"Oh, yes, I won't fail to attend."

"Your colleague, Miss Bassett, always carries a large pincushion on such occasions. The minister must have at least five of her manufacture."

"In that case," said Mabel, smiling, "I think I will choose a different gift."

CHAPTER SEVEN

A few evenings later, at Mrs. Pratt's house, Mabel met an individual of whom she had frequently heard since her arrival in Granville. This was Mr. Randolph Chester, a bachelor from New York, who generally passed part of the summer in the village. He was reputed to be rich, and, though his wealth was exaggerated, he actually had enough to support a single man in comfort and even luxury. Though a bachelor, he allowed it to be understood that he was in the matrimonial market, and thus received no little attention from maneuvering mothers, single ladies of uncertain age, and blooming maidens who were willing to overlook disparity in age for the sake of wealth and position which it was understood Mr. Chester would be able to give them.

Why did Mr. Randolph Chester (he liked to be called by his full name) summer in Granville when he might have gone to Bar Harbor or Newport? Because at these places of resort he would have been nobody, while in a small New Hampshire village he was a great man. In Granville he felt, though in this he was perhaps mistaken, that he could marry any of the village belles to whom he chose to hold out his finger, and this consciousness was flattering.

On his arrival at the hotel, where he had a special room reserved for him summer after summer, he was told of the new school teacher, a young, beautiful, and accomplished girl from New York.

"If I like her looks," thought he to himself, "I may marry her. Of course she's poor, or she wouldn't be teaching here for the paltry wages of a country school mistress, and she'll be glad enough to accept me."

When he was introduced to her Mabel saw before her a middle aged man, carefully dressed, passably good looking, and evidently very well pleased with himself. On his part, he was somewhat dazzled by the school teacher's attractions.

"Why, the girl has actual style," he said to himself. "Egad, she would appear to advantage in a New York drawing room. I wonder if she's heard about me."

He felt doubtful on this point, for Mabel received him with well bred indifference. He missed the little flutter of gratified vanity which the attentions of such an eligible *parti* usually produced in the young ladies of Granville.

"I believe you are from New York, my own city," he said complacently.

"I have passed some time there."

"You must—ahem!—find a considerable difference between the city and this village."

"Undoubtedly, Mr. Chester. I find it a pleasant relief to be here."

"To be sure. So do I. I enjoy leaving the gay saloons of New York for the green glades of the country."

"I can't say," returned Mabel mischievously, "that I know much about the saloons of New York."

"Of course I mean the saloons of fashion—the shining circles of gay society," said Mr. Chester hastily, half suspecting that she was laughing at him. "Do you know the Livingstons, Miss Frost?"

"There is a baker of that name on Sixth Avenue, I believe," said Mabel innocently. "Do you mean his family?"

"No, certainly not," said Mr. Randolph Chester, quite shocked at the idea. "I haven't the honor of knowing any baker on Sixth Avenue."

Neither had Mabel, but she had fully made up her mind to tease Mr. Randolph Chester, whose self conceit she instinctively divined.

"Then you don't live on Sixth Avenue," she continued. "I wonder where I got that impression!"

"Certainly not," said Mr. Chester, scandalized. "I have apartments on Madison Avenue."

"I know where it is," said Mabel.

"She can't move in any sort of society, and yet where on earth did she get that air of distinction?" Randolph Chester reflected. "Do you like school teaching?" he asked in a patronizing tone.

"I find it pleasant."

"I wonder you do not procure a position in the city, where you could obtain higher wages."

"Do you think I could?" asked Mabel.

"My friend, Mr. Livingston, is one of the School Commissioners," said Mr. Chester. "I can mention your name to him, and you might stand a chance to obtain the next vacancy."

"Thank you, Mr. Chester, you are exceedingly kind, but I don't think that I wish to become a candidate at present."

"But you are really throwing away your talents in a small country village like this."

"I don't think so," said Mabel. "I find many of my scholars pretty intelligent, and it is a real pleasure to guide them."

"Mr. Randolph Chester, you mustn't try to lure away Miss Frost. We can't spare her," said Mrs. Pratt.

"You see, Mr. Chester, that I am appreciated here," said Mabel. "In the city I might not be."

"I think," said the bachelor gallantly, "that you would be appreciated anywhere."

"Thank you, Mr. Chester," returned Mabel, receiving the compliment without seeming at all overpowered by it; "but you see you speak from a very short acquaintance."

Mr. Randolph Chester was piqued. He felt that his attentions were not estimated at their real value. The school mistress could not understand what an eligible *parti* he was.

"Do you propose to remain here after the summer is over, Miss Frost?" he asked.

"My plans are quite undecided," said Mabel.

"I suppose she isn't sure whether she can secure the school for the fall term," thought the bachelor.

There was a piano in the room, recently purchased for Carrie Pratt, Mrs. Pratt's daughter.

"I wonder whether she plays," thought Mr. Chester. "Will you give us some music, Miss Frost?" he asked.

"If you desire it. What is your taste?"

"Do you know any operatic airs?"

"A few"; and Mabel began with an air from "La Sonnambula." She played with a dash and execution which Mr. Chester recognized, though he only pretended to like opera because it was fashionable.

"Bravó!" he exclaimed, clapping his hands in affected ecstasy. "Really you are an excellent player. I suppose you have attended the opera?"

"Occasionally," said Mabel.

"And you like music? But I need not ask."

"Oh, yes, I like music. It is one of my greatest pleasures."

"You would make a very successful music teacher, I should judge. I should think you would prefer it to teaching a country school."

"I like music too well to teach it. I am afraid that I should find it drudgery to initiate beginners."

"There may be something in that."

"Do you sing, Miss Frost?" asked Mrs. Pratt.

"Sometimes."

"Will you sing something, to oblige me?"

"Certainly, Mrs. Pratt. What would you like?"

"I like ballad music. I am afraid my ear is not sufficiently trained to like operatic airs, such as Mr. Randolph Chester admires."

After a brief prelude Mabel sang an old ballad. Her voice was very flexible, and was not wanting in strength. It was very easy to see that it had been carefully cultivated.

Mr. Chester was more and more surprised and charmed. "That girl is quite out of place here," he said to himself. "Any commonplace girl would do for the Granville school mistress. She deserves a more brilliant position."

He surveyed Mabel critically, but could find no fault with her appearance. She was beautiful, accomplished, and had a distinguished air. Even if she were related to the baker's family on Sixth Avenue, as he thought quite probable, she was fitted to adorn the "saloons of fashion," as he called them.

"I rather think I will marry her," he thought. "I don't believe I can do better. She is poor, to be sure, but I have enough for both, and can raise her to my own position in society."

Fortunately Mabel did not know what was passing through the

mind of the antiquated beau, as she regarded him, who amused her by his complacent consciousness of his superiority. When it was ten o'clock, she rose to go.

"It won't do to be dissipated, Mrs. Pratt," she said. "I must be going home."

"Permit me to escort you, Miss Frost," said Mr. Chester, rising with alacrity.

She hesitated, but could think of no reason for declining, and they walked together to Mrs. Kent's. The distance was short—too short, Mr. Chester thought, but there was no way of lengthening it.

"I hope to have the pleasure of meeting you again soon, Miss Frost," said the bachelor at parting.

Mabel responded in suitable terms, and Mr. Randolph Chester went back to the hotel in quite a flutter of excitement. The staid bachelor was as nearly in love as such a well regulated person could be.

The next evening Mabel spent in writing a letter to Mary Bridgman, part of which it may be well to quote.

"You," she said, "are the only person in my confidence, the only one who knows of my present whereabouts. You will, I feel sure, be glad to know that my experiment is proving to be a success. I believe I have inspired in my pupils a real and earnest interest in study. It gives me genuine pleasure to see their minds unfolding and expanding, day by day, and to feel that I am doing an important part in guiding them in this intellectual growth. I can assure you that I get more satisfaction and exhilaration from the life I am leading now than I found in my last summer's round of amusements at Newport.

"When will it end? How long will this fit of enthusiasm last? If you ask these questions, I cannot tell you. Let time decide.

"You have heard, I suppose, of Mr. Randolph Chester, the elderly bachelor who favors Granville with his presence every summer. I made his acquaintance yesterday, while calling upon Mrs. Pratt. His air of condescension on being introduced to the school teacher was very amusing. He was evidently disappointed by my indifference, and seemed piqued by it. When I was asked to play I determined to produce an impression upon him, and I did my best. Mr. Chester seemed surprised to find a country school mistress so accomplished. He recommended me to become a music teacher and offered to assist me to obtain a position in the city, professing to regard me worthy of a larger field than Granville affords. He offered his escort home, and I accepted.

"Today Mr. Chester did me the great honor of visiting my school. He professed a great interest in the subject of education, but I learn, on inquiry, that he has never before visited the school. I suggested to him that Miss Bassett would be glad to receive a call; but he shrugged his shoulders and did not welcome the proposal. I felt a malicious satisfaction in introducing him publicly to my scholars as one who took a strong interest in them, and announced that he would address them. My visitor started, blushed, and looked embarrassed, but retreat was impossible. He made a halting speech, chiefly consisting of congratulations to the scholars upon having so accomplished and capable a teacher. On the whole he rather turned the tables upon me.

"It is quite in the line of possibility that I may have a chance to become Mrs. Randolph Chester before the season is over. If I accept him I shall insist on your being one of my bridesmaids."

CHAPTER EIGHT

Granville was not on the great highway of travel. It was off the track of the ordinary tourist. Yet now and then a pilgrim in search of a quiet nook, where there was nothing to suggest the great Babel of fashion, came to anchor in its modest hostelry, and dreamed away tranquil hours under the shadow of its leafy elms. Occasionally, in her walks to and from school, Mabel noticed a face which seemed less at home in village lanes than in city streets, but none that she had seen before.

"I shall finish my summer experiment without recognition," she said to herself in a tone of gratulation. But she was mistaken.

Within a few rods from the school house, one afternoon, she met a young man armed with a fishing rod. He was of medium height, broad shouldered, wore a brown beard, and had a pleasant, manly face lighted up by clear and expressive eyes. To Mabel's casual glance his features looked strangely familiar, but she could not recall the circumstances under which they had met.

The stranger looked doubtfully in her face for an instant, then his countenance brightened up.

"If I am not mistaken," he said eagerly, "it is Miss Mabel Fairfax."

Mabel, at the sound of her real name, looked around uneasily, but luckily none of her scholars was within hearing.

"Mabel Frost," she said hurriedly.

"I beg pardon," replied the young man, puzzled; "but can I be mistaken?"

"No, you are right; but please forget the name you have called me by. Here I am Mabel Frost, and I teach the village school."

There was a look of wonder, mingled with sympathy, in the young man's face.

"I understand," he said gently. "You have been unfortunate; you have lost your fortune, and you have buried yourself in this out of the way village."

Mabel preferred that he should accept the explanation that he himself had suggested.

"Do not pity me," she said. "I have no cause to complain. I am happy here."

"How well you bear your reverses!" he replied admiringly.

Mabel felt like a humbug; but it was a necessary consequence of the false position in which she had placed herself.

"I do not deserve your praise," she said honestly. "I am sure I ought to know you," she added. "Your face is familiar, but I cannot recall where we have met."

"That is not surprising," he returned. "I am a painter, and you met me at the artists' reception. My name is Allan Thorpe."

"Allan Thorpe!" repeated Mabel with a glow of pleasure. "Yes, I remember, you painted that beautiful 'Sunset in Bethlehem.'"

"Do you remember it?" asked the artist in gratified surprise.

"It was one of the pictures I like best. I remember you too, Mr. Thorpe."

"I am very glad to her it, Miss——"

"Frost," prompted Mabel, holding up her finger.

"I will try to remember."

"Are you spending the summer in Granville, Mr. Thorpe?"

"Yes," replied Allan unhesitatingly. He had just made up his mind.

"Are you engaged upon any new work?"

"Not yet. I have been painting busily during the spring, and am idling for a time. You see how profitably I have been employed today," and he pointed to his fishing rod. "I hope to get at something by and by. May I ask where you are boarding?"

"At Mrs. Kent's."

"I congratulate you, for I know her. I am at the hotel and am sometimes solitary. May I venture to call upon you?"

"If you call upon your friend, Mrs. Kent, you will probably see me," said Mabel, smiling.

"Then I shall certainly call upon Mrs. Kent," said the young man, lifting his hat respectfully.

"Please bear in mind my change of name, Mr. Thorpe."

"You shall be obeyed."

"How much she is improved by adversity," thought the young man, as he sauntered towards the hotel. "I can hardly realize the change. The society belle has become a staid—no, not staid, but hard working country school mistress, and takes the change gayly and cheerfully. I thought her beautiful when I saw her in New York. Now she is charming."

What were Mabel's reflections?

"He is certainly very handsome and very manly," she said to herself. "He has genius, too. I remember that painting of his. He thinks me poor, and I felt like a humbug when he was admiring me for my resignation to circumstances. If it were as he thinks, I think I might find a friend in him."

"I just met an old acquaintance, Mrs. Kent," she said on entering the house.

"Is he staying here?" asked the widow.

"Yes, for a time. He tells me he knows you."

"Who can it be?" asked Mrs. Kent with interest.

"A young artist—Allan Thorpe," replied Mabel.

"He is a fine young man," said Mrs. Kent warmly.

"His appearance is in his favor."

"You know, I suppose, that he is Mrs. Wilson's nephew?"

"No," said Mabel with surprise.

"His mother, who died last year, was Mrs. Wilson's sister. He was a good son to her. A year before her death a wealthy friend offered to defray his expenses for twelve months in Italy, but he refused for her sake, though it has always been his dearest wish to go."

"No wonder you praise him. He deserves it," said Mabel warmly.

CHAPTER NINE

Three months before, a new minister had been appointed to take charge of the Methodist Society in Granville. The Rev. Adoniram Fry, in spite of an unprepossessing name, was a man of liberal mind and genial temper, who could neither originate nor keep up a quarrel. In consequence the relations between the two parishes became much more friendly. Mr. Fry took the initiative in calling upon Mr. Wilson.

"Brother Wilson," he said cordially, "we are both laborers in the Lord's vineyard. Is there any reason why we should stand apart?"

"None whatever, Brother Fry," said the other clergyman, his face lighting up with pleasure. "Let us be friends."

"Agreed. If we set the example we can draw our people together. How is it that they have been estranged in years past?"

"I can hardly tell you. Probably there has been fault on both sides."

The two pastors had a pleasant chat, and walked together down the village street, attracting considerable attention. Some were pleased, others seemed undecided how to regard the new alliance, while Deacon Uriah Peabody openly disapproved.

"I don't believe in countenancin' error," said he, shaking his head. "We should be stern and uncompromisin' in upholding the right."

"Why shouldn't our minister be friendly with the Methodist parson, deacon?" questioned Squire Hadley, who was less bigoted than the deacon. "I've met Mr. Fry, and I think him a whole souled man."

"He may have a whole soul," retorted the deacon, with grim humor; "but it's a question whether he'll save it if he holds to his Methodist doctrines."

"Don't the Methodists and Congregationalists believe very much alike?" asked the Squire.

"How can you ask such a question, Squire?" asked the deacon, scandalized.

"But how do they differ? I wish you'd tell me that."

"The Methodists have bishops."

"That isn't a matter of doctrine."

"Yes, it is; they say it's accordin' to Scripture to have bishops."

"Is that all the difference?"

"It's enough."

"Enough to prevent their being saved?"

"It's an error, and all error is dangerous."

"Then you disapprove of friendship between our people and the Methodists?"

"Yes," said the deacon emphatically.

"Wouldn't you sell a cow to a Methodist if you could get a good profit?"

"That's different," said Deacon Peabody, who was fond of a trade. "Tradin' is one thing and spiritual intercourse is another."

"I can't agree with you, deacon. I like what I've seen of Mr. Fry, and I hope he'll draw us together in friendly feeling without regard to our attendance at different churches."

When Fast Day came Mr. Wilson proposed that there should be a union service in the Methodist church, Mr. Fry to preach the sermon.

"In the two societies," he urged, "there will not be enough people desirous of attending church to make more than a fair sized congregation. Nothing sectarian need be preached. There are doctrines enough in which we jointly believe to afford the preacher all the scope he needs."

Mr. Fry cordially accepted the suggestion, and the union service was held; but Deacon Uriah Peabody was conspicuous by his absence.

"I don't like to lose my gospel privileges," he said; "but I can't consort with Methodists or enter a Methodist church. It's agin' my principles."

Old Mrs. Slocum sympathized with the deacon; but curiosity got the better of principle, and she attended the service, listening with keen eared and vigilant attention for something with which she could disagree. In this she was disappointed; there was nothing to startle or shock the most exacting Congregationalist.

"What did you think of the sermon?" asked Squire Hadley, as he fell in with the old lady on the way home.

"It sounded well enough," she replied, shaking her head; "but appearances are deceitful."

"Would you have been satisfied if you had heard the same sermon from Mr. Wilson?"

"I would have known it was all right then," said Mrs. Slocum. "You can't never tell about these Methodists."

But Deacon Peabody and Mrs. Slocum were exceptions. Most of the people were satisfied, and the union service led to a more social and harmonious feeling. For the first time in three years Mrs. John Keith, Congregationalist, took tea at the house of Mrs. Henry Keith, Methodist. The two families, though the husbands were brothers, had been kept apart by sectarian differences, each being prominent in his church. The two ministers rejoiced in the more cordial feeling which had grown out of their own pleasant personal relations, and they frequently called upon each other.

One result of the restored harmony between the two religious societies was a union picnic of the Sunday schools connected with each. It became a general affair, and it was understood that not only the children, but the older people, would participate in it. The place selected was a grove on the summit of a little hill sloping down to Thurber's Pond, a sheet of water sometimes designated as a lake, though scarcely a mile in circumference.

From the first, Mr. Randolph Chester intended to invite Mabel to accompany him. The attention would look pointed, he admitted to himself; but he was quite prepared for that. So far as his heart was capable of being touched Mabel had touched it. He was not the man to entertain a grand passion, and never had been; but his admiration of the new school teacher was such that a refusal would have entailed upon him serious disappointment. Of rivalry—that is, of serious rivalry—Mr. Chester had no apprehension. One afternoon he encountered Allan Thorpe walking with Mabel, and he was not quite pleased, for he had mentally monopolized her. But he would have laughed at the idea of Mabel's preferring Mr. Thorpe. He was handsome, and younger by twenty five years; but he was, to use Mr. Chester's own term, "a beggarly artist."

"If she should marry Thorpe she would have to live on romance and moonshine. Artists rave about the true and the beautiful, but they do not pay cash," Randolph said to himself, rather disdainfully.

Two days before the picnic Mr. Chester called at Mrs. Kent's and inquired, in a tone of some importance, for Miss Frost. Mabel made her appearance in the parlor without unnecessary delay.

"I hope I see you well, Miss Frost," said Mr. Chester, with a smile that was meant to be captivating.

"Thank you, Mr. Chester; I have seldom been better."

"I hope you are enjoying your summer in Granville."

"Indeed I am," answered Mabel heartily.

"Where were you last summer, Miss Frost?"

Mabel hesitated. She did not like to say that she spent the greater part of the season at Newport, since this would probably lead to further questions on the subject, and possibly expose her secret.

"I was in the city part of the time," she answered evasively.

"It must have been very uncomfortable," said Mr. Chester,

adding complacently: "I have never passed the summer in New York. I should find it quite intolerable."

"A rich man can consult his own wishes," said Mabel. "If you were a poor school teacher it would be different."

Randolph Chester always enjoyed allusions to his wealth. It gratified him that Mabel seemed aware of his easy circumstances.

"Quite true, Miss Frost," he answered. "I often feel how fortunate I am in my worldly circumstances. You ought to be rich," he continued. "You have accomplishments which would grace a high social position."

"I am afraid you flatter me, Mr. Chester."

"Upon my word I do not," said the bachelor warmly. He was dangerously near declaring himself, but stopped upon the brink. He did not wish to be precipitate.

"Are you going to the picnic on Saturday, Miss Frost?"

"I believe so. Everybody will go, and I do not want to be out of fashion."

"Permit me to offer my escort," said Randolph Chester gallantly.

"You are too late, Mr. Chester," said Mabel, with a smile. "Some one has already invited me."

"Indeed!" said the bachelor stiffly, and looking offended. "May I inquire who that somebody is?"

"Certainly; it is no secret. I have promised to accompany Mr. Allan Thorpe."

"Oh! The artist!"

The words were few, but the tone spoke volumes. It expressed disdain, and implied that to be an artist was something exceedingly disreputable.

"Yes," said Mabel, not unwilling to tease her elderly admirer, "as you say, he is an artist. He paints very clever pictures. Have you ever seen any of them, Mr. Chester?"

"Can't say I have," answered Mr. Chester shortly.

"He promises to be eminent some day," continued Mabel.

"Does he? A good many promises are unfulfilled. I don't think much of artists."

"How can you say that, Mr. Chester? I thought every man of culture admired the pictures of Titian and Raphael."

"Of course," said Mr. Chester, suspecting that he had gone too far. "They are the old masters, you know. It's the modern daubers of canvas that I was speaking of."

"But are not some of the artists of the present day to become eminent?" asked Mabel.

"When they have become so I will admire them. I don't think Mr. Thorpe stands much chance of it if he wastes his time in Granville."

"Then you don't know that he is painting a picture here?"

"I know nothing of the young man's movements," said Mr. Randolph Chester loftily. "Then I shall not have the pleasure of escorting you, Miss Frost?"

"I fear not. I hope, however, to meet you there."

"I am not sure that I shall go," returned Mr. Chester discontentedly.

"I believe Miss Bassett is unprovided with an escort, Mr. Chester," suggested Mabel, still bent on teasing him.

"I don't care to escort a Maypole," said the bachelor quickly. "Miss Bassett is not to my taste."

"I am afraid you are very fastidious, Mr. Chester."

"I admit that I am so. I prefer to leave Miss Clarissa to some one who appreciates her more than I do."

Soon after Randolph Chester took his leave. He went from the presence of Mabel in a very uncomfortable frame of mind. His feelings toward the artist were far from cordial.

"Why couldn't he go somewhere else?" soliloquized Mr. Chester. "I am sure nobody wanted him here." But the idea would intrude itself that perhaps Miss Frost wanted him. He would not entertain it. "She is like all the girls," he reflected. "She is trying to bring me to the point. So she is playing off the beggarly artist against me. I wish I could retaliate. If I could find some other girl to take I might make her jealous."

This struck Mr. Chester as a happy thought. But whom could he select? There was Clarissa Bassett: but no girl in her sober senses would think of being jealous of *her*. Still undecided, Mr. Chester reached the hotel, when, to his satisfaction, he found the Raymonds, of Brooklyn, had arrived to spend a couple of weeks there for recreation.

The Raymonds included Mrs. Raymond and her two daughters. The elder was a girl of twenty-four, not pretty, but with plenty of pretension. The younger, ten years younger, was still a school girl. The family was supposed to occupy a very exalted social position. All that was known on the subject in Granville came from themselves, and surely they ought to know. They were constantly making references to their aristocratic acquaintances and connections, and evidently felt that in visiting Granville they were conferring a marked favor on that obscure place.

Randolph Chester had not a particle of admiration for Clementina Raymond, but he hailed her arrival with great satisfaction. She was quite a different person from Clarissa Bassett. He would invite her to the picnic and pay her marked attention. Thus, he did not doubt, he could arouse the jealousy of Mabel, and punish her for accepting the escort of Allan Thorpe.

"I am delighted to see you, Miss Raymond," he said.

Clementina received him very graciously. She understood that he was an eligible *parti,* and she had not found suitors plentiful. The Raymonds encouraged the idea that they were very rich, but it was a fiction. They were, in truth, considerably straitened, and this probably accounted for their selecting, as a summer home, the modest hotel at Granville, where for seven dollars a week they could live better than they allowed themselves to do at home, and keep up their social status by being "out of town." Clementina not only desired to marry, but to marry a man of means, and it was understood that Mr. Randolph Chester was rich. He must be nearly fifty, to be sure, while she was only twenty-four; but this would not prove an insuperable objection to the match.

"How long have you been here, Mr. Chester?" asked Miss Raymond languidly.

"Two weeks or more, Miss Raymond. I began to fear you would overlook Granville this summer."

"We had half a mind to go to Newport," said Clementina. "So many of our set there, you know. But mamma likes quiet, and preferred to come here. The rest of the year, I am *so* gay—I am sure you know what a tyrant society is—that with balls, parties, and receptions, I was really quite run down, and our physician strongly advised some quiet place like this. I was afraid of being bored, but since you are here, Mr. Chester, I feel quite encouraged."

Mr. Chester cared nothing for Miss Raymond, but he did like flattery, and he was pleased with this compliment.

"I am quite at your service, Miss Raymond," he responded cheerfully. "You won't find in Granville the gayety of Brooklyn or New York, but we have our amusements. For instance, day after tomorrow there is to be a union picnic at Thurber's Pond."

"How charming! I shall certainly go; that is, if ladies can go unattended."

"That will be quite *en regle,* but if you will accept my escort, Miss Raymond——"

"I shall be delighted, Mr. Chester, I am sure. May mamma go too?"

"Certainly," said Mr. Chester, but he did not look delighted.

"My dear," said the thoughtful mother, "I hardly feel equal to remaining there all the afternoon. You go with Mr. Chester, since he is so kind as to invite you. I may appear there in the course of the afternoon."

"Since you prefer it, I will, mamma," said Clementina softly. No daughter was more filial and considerate than she—in public.

Mabel was with Allan Thorpe, watching the amusements of the children, when she recognized Mr. Randolph Chester approaching. By his side walked Miss Clementina, a stately figure, overtopping her escort.

"Who is that lady with Mr. Chester?" she asked, in some curiosity.

"Miss Raymond, of Brooklyn," replied Thorpe. "The Raymonds are at the hotel."

"She seems to be a young lady of some pretension," remarked Mabel, rather amused by Clementina's airs.

"Quite so," said Mr. Thorpe. "She is a person of very considerable importance—in her own eyes."

"You may be in danger, Mr. Thorpe; I believe you are fellow boarders."

"The danger is slight; Miss Clementina regards me as a poor artist, quite unworthy of her attentions. Occasionally she condescends to notice me; but in her eyes, I am an inferior being."

"I fancy I shall be classed in the same category when she learns that I am the village school mistress."

"I suspect you are right. Will it materially detract from your enjoyment, Miss Frost, if this proves to be so?"

Mabel laughed merrily.

"I have considerable fortitude," she replied, "and I hope to bear up under it. See, they are coming this way."

Randolph Chester had not failed to notice Mabel, and it caused him a pang of jealousy to see her under the escort of another. He meant that she should see him, and, with Miss Raymond by his side, advanced to where they were standing.

"Oh, this is Miss Frost, the new teacher," he said. "Let me introduce you."

"I believe you are a teacher, Miss Frost," said Clementina, when this formality had been accomplished.

"I teach the grammar school in this village, Miss Raymond," replied Mabel demurely.

"A very useful vocation," remarked Miss Raymond patronizingly. "I really feel ashamed of myself when I compare myself with you. I am afraid we fashionable girls are very useless."

"Not necessarily so. Your means of usefulness are greater," replied Mabel.

"To be sure. We contribute to charities, and all that, but it isn't like taking part in the work."

It would probably be extremely difficult to discover any charities that were materially assisted by Miss Raymond, but it suited her to convey the impression that she gave liberally.

"I agree with you, Miss Raymond," said Allan Thorpe, speaking for the first time. "It is not enough to give money."

"I plead quilty, Mr. Thorpe," said Clementina, ready to charge herself with any sin that was fashionable; "but really, if you only knew how hard society girls find it to give their time—there are so many claims upon us—parties, receptions, the opera. Oh, I know what you will say. We should sacrifice our inclinations, and steal time to do good. I dare say you think so, Miss Frost."

"It seems to me that it would become a pleasure as well as a duty to do something for others."

"Excuse me, Miss Frost, but you cannot tell till you are placed as I am."

"Possibly not."

All this was very amusing to Mabel. She strongly suspected that Miss Raymond's claims to high social position would not bear examination. It was a novel sensation to be treated as one who had no knowledge of the great world from which she had voluntarily exiled herself, and she had no desire to disturb Miss Raymond in her delusion. Mr. Thorpe also enjoyed the scene. Though he believed her to be in reduced circumstances, he had seen her playing a brilliant part in New

York society, and he was equally confident that Miss Raymond was a social humbug.

"Shall we promenade, Mr. Chester?" asked Clementina.

"If you desire it," said her escort, with a show of devotion intended to create uneasiness in Mabel.

"May I come to your school some day, Miss Frost?" asked Miss Raymond. "I should like to visit a country school."

"I shall be glad to see you," said Mabel politely.

"Thank you so much. I will come if I can induce Mr. Randolph Chester to accompany me."

"Mr. Chester has already favored me with a visit," said Mabel, smiling.

Clementina glanced suspiciously at her escort. Was it possible that he felt an interest in the school teacher?

"You will let him come again?" she asked, smiling sweetly.

"Most certainly."

"What do you think of her?" asked Mr. Chester with peculiar interest, after the two couples had separated.

"I rather like her appearance," drawled Clementina slightingly, "but you know there is always something plebeian about people of her class, however they may dress."

"I can't quite agree with you, Miss Raymond," said the bachelor, who did not like to hear the future Mrs. Randolph Chester spoken of in such contemptuous terms. "Miss Mabel Frost is from the city of New York, and is a highly accomplished girl. I suspect she has seen better days, though at present reduced to school teaching."

Clementina was quick witted, and saw how the land lay. Having resolved to capture the gentleman at her side, she determined to check his evident admiration for Mabel.

"Mr. Chester," she said, "I don't wonder you are deceived. The girl has a superficial polish, which a gentleman is not likely to see through. I have been a great deal in society, and can at once distinguish the counterfeit from the genuine. This school teacher has probably received more than ordinary advantages; but blood will tell. Rely upon it, she is a plebeian."

Mr. Chester did not think any the better of his companion for this speech. He was too deeply interested in Mabel, and as strong as ever in the determination to make her Mrs. Chester.

"I fancy that this Mr. Thorpe is very devoted to her," continued Clementina.

"I didn't notice it," replied Mr. Chester shortly.

"But the devotion was very marked, and I am quite disposed to think it was mutual. Did you ever think, Mr. Chester, how interesting it is to study love making between people of their class? And really, when you come to think of it," she rattled on, much to the disgust of her escort, "it would be a capital match. He is a poor artist, you know, and they would have to live in a *very* modest style, but she is used to that. I do not suppose she would object to doing her own work, and of course she would be obliged to do so at first. I hope they will invite us to the wedding."

"I don't believe there will be any wedding," said Mr. Chester uncomfortably. "He is only paying her a little ordinary attention. She wouldn't accept him, I am confident."

"Why wouldn't she? She can't expect a husband in *your* position, for instance, Mr. Chester. She probably has low relations, and it wouldn't be suitable or pleasant."

Mr. Chester thought of the baker on Sixth Avenue; but the time had passed when even that could deter him. In spite of all that Miss Raymond could suggest his mind was made up.

CHAPTER TEN

Thurber's Pond was of moderate size, probably covering thirty or forty acres. Near the edge it was shallow, but toward the middle the water was of considerable depth. There were two boats moored at the little pier built out at the foot of the picnic grounds, one a sail boat and the other a row boat.

Toward the middle of the afternoon it was proposed to press these boats into the service of some of the older visitors. The children were scattered through the neighboring fields, playing games that interested them. The sail boat proved the more attractive, and was already full before Mabel, Clementina, and their escorts became aware of the plan proposed.

Clementina was very much annoyed.

"It's so provoking," she complained. "I dote on the water. Isn't there room for me?"

But the sail boat was, if anything, too full already, and nobody offered to get out. Allan Thorpe and Mabel were standing by, both a little disappointed. The artist's eye fell upon the row boat.

"Do you row, Mr. Chester?" he asked.

"A little," was the answer.

"Then suppose, since we are unable to go in the sail boat, we give the ladies a row. Would you like it, Miss Frost?"

"Thank you," said Mabel. "I should enjoy it very much."

"And you, Miss Raymond?"

"It will be better than moping here."

So the four seated themselves in the boat, and the gentlemen took up the oars. Mr. Chester proved to be very awkward, and Allan Thorpe offered to row alone. The bachelor accepted with alacrity, and seated himself next to Mabel, leaving Miss Raymond at the other end of the boat. This did not suit Clementina, who straightway lost her interest in the excursion. She felt herself ill used at this act of desertion on the part of her escort. Mabel read her discontent, and wanted to suggest to Mr. Chester that she could dispense with his company, but this was difficult to do. His face beamed with satisfaction, and Miss Raymond saw it, and was provoked. She even deigned to be jealous of the school mistress.

"You are not very considerate, Mr. Chester," she said sharply, "in leaving Mr. Thorpe to do all the work."

"He likes it," replied Randolph lazily. "Don't you Mr. Thorpe?"

"I always enjoy rowing," said Allan, who understood very well that Mr. Chester could not manage both oars.

"I would rather look on," continued Chester contentedly. "How are you getting on with your school, Miss Frost?"

"Very well, thank you."

"I wish I was young enough to enroll myself among your scholars," said the bachelor gallantly.

"You would find me very strict, Mr. Chester."

"I should take care not to give you any trouble."

Miss Raymond did not enjoy this badinage, and mentally pronounced Mabel an artful girl, who had designs upon Mr. Chester's affections. She could not resist the temptation to revenge herself on her escort.

"I suppose you can hardly remember your school days, Mr. Chester?" said she.

"Really, Miss Raymond, I am not quite an antediluvian," exclaimed Randolph Chester, somewhat provoked.

"Excuse me, Mr. Chester. I didn't suppose you were sensitive about your age. I really hope you'll excuse me."

"I do not know that I have any reason to be sensitive *as yet,*" said Mr. Chester stiffly. "It will be time enough for that when I reach fifty."

He was that already; but this was a secret between himself and the old Bible, which neither of his hearers was likely to have a chance of seeing.

Clementina's purpose was achieved. She had made Mr. Chester uncomfortable, and interrupted his tête-à-tête with Mabel. She followed up her advantage by becoming very sociable with Allan Thorpe.

"Are you at work upon another charming picture, Mr. Thorpe?" she asked graciously.

"You are very kind, Miss Raymond; I am painting another picture. I hope it may deserve the adjective you use."

"I like your paintings *so* much. Have you ever been to Italy?"

"No," said Mr. Thorpe regretfully. "I wish I could go."

"You really ought to do so. I adore art myself. I should like nothing better than to see the grand Italian galleries, with some one to point out the best pictures—some one like yourself, who understands the subject."

"Have you ever been abroad, Miss Raymond?" asked Mabel.

"No," said Clementina. "Mamma has such a horror of the sea; she is so liable to be seasick. It is such a pity, when one has the means, that there should be a drawback."

This was another of Clementina's little fictions. In plain truth, want of means was the only objection to a European trip on the part of the Raymonds.

"When you are married, Miss Raymond, you will not be dependent on your mother as a companion; then you can gratify your taste."

"So I can," said Clementina with naïve simplicity, as if the idea had just occurred to her. "If I can't go in any other way, I shall be willing to pay the expenses of the tour myself. So you're really at work upon a new picture, Mr. Thorpe?"

"I have not made much progress yet, but I have made a beginning."

"I should like to see it. I couldn't, of course, hope to offer any suggestion, but I can tell whether I like it."

"Thank you. When it is more advanced I shall be glad to ask your opinion of it."

"Do you ever give lessons in painting, Mr. Thorpe?"

"I did at one time, but I found that it interfered with my work."

"Then I cannot hope to secure you as a teacher. It would be so nice to go out in the fields, and take lessons from so competent an instructor."

"You flatter me, Miss Raymond."

"You only say so because of your modesty, Mr. Thorpe. I have a high opinion of your talent, and I shall take every opportunity of mentioning you in my set."

"Thank you."

Allan Thorpe was clear sighted enough to estimate Miss Raymond's sudden interest in him at its right value. He also had a suspicion that her set was not one likely to care much for arts or artists. But it amused him to watch Clementina's jealousy, and to penetrate her motives in turning her attention to him.

"If I can help her to secure a husband," he thought, "she is quite welcome to make use of me."

It did not seem, however, that she had accomplished much. Mr. Chester was chatting contentedly with Mabel, glad that Clementina was otherwise occupied than in teasing him.

"Then you are not sure that you will remain in Granville after the summer, Miss Frost?" he inquired.

"My plans are quite undecided," answered Mabel.

"I suppose you will continue to teach?"

"Even that is not certain. Perhaps I might obtain a situation as companion to an elderly lady. Do you know of any likely to want my services, Mr. Chester?"

Mr. Chester would have liked to suggest that the position of companion to a gentleman was open to her acceptance; but the occasion was too public.

"I may hear of such a position, Miss Frost," he said; "and if you will leave me your address, in case you do not remain in Granville, I will certainly let you know."

"Thank you, Mr. Chester."

At this point there was a startling interruption. Miss Raymond had been sitting for five minutes silent and incensed. Her little flirtation with Mr. Thorpe had not ruffled Mr. Chester's serenity nor interrupted his devotion to the school mistress. She rose from her seat, lost her balance, and fell against the side of the boat, upsetting it, and precipitating the four who occupied it into the water.

Fortunately they were not far from shore. Still, the water was six feet deep, and of course there was danger. Mr. Chester could swim a little, and, without a thought of his companions, he struck out for the shore. Allan Thorpe could swim also. Fortunately he was cool in the moment of peril. His first thought was for Mabel.

"Cling to me, Mabel," he said, forgetting ceremony at this moment. "I will help you."

Clementina, wild with terror, had grasped him by the coat, and this hampered his movements; but with a great effort, he succeeded in conveying both girls to more shallow water. Had the distance been greater, it is doubtful if he would have succeeded.

"You are out of danger," he said. "The water is not deep here. We can walk ashore."

Randolph Chester, still a little pale, was dripping on the bank when Allan and the two girls joined him.

"I am so glad you are safe, ladies," he said a little sheepishly, for he was conscious that he had not played a heroic part.

"Small thanks to you, Mr. Chester!" retorted Clementina sharply. "We might have drowned, so far as you were concerned."

"I cannot swim much," said Mr. Chester uneasily. "I never regretted it so much as now."

"You could swim well enough to save yourself. Mr. Thorpe, you are my preserver!" exclaimed Clementina gushingly.

"Do not magnify my service, Miss Raymond. We were very near shoal water."

"But you saved my life," persisted Clementina. "I shall *never* forget it."

Mabel said nothing, but she impulsively extended her hand. Allan Thorpe was better pleased than with Miss Raymond's demonstrative expressions of gratitude.

"Now, young ladies," said the artist, "though I am no physician, you must allow me to prescribe an immediate return home. Otherwise you'll run a great risk of catching cold. Mr. Chester, if you will take charge of Miss Raymond, I will accompany Miss Frost. For your own sake, you will find it best to go at once."

Miss Raymond was rather sulky, but, though irritated with her escort, policy prevailed, and she forced herself into a good humor. She had made up her mind to marry Mr. Chester, and he required delicate management. So she accepted the lame apology he offered for leaving her to her fate, and by the time they reached the hotel they were outwardly on good terms.

On the day after the picnic, Allan Thorpe wrote the following letter to his friend and fellow artist John Fleming, who was spending the summer at Bethlehem:

> Dear Jack
>
> You wonder why I prefer to spend the summer at Granville, and refuse to join you at Bethlehem. Your surprise is natural. I admit that between Granville and Bethlehem there is no comparison. The latter is certainly far more attractive to an artist who has only his art in view. But, Jack, there is another reason. You were always my father confessor—at least you have been since the happy day when our friendship began—and I am willing to confess to you that I have lost my heart. There is a charming school mistress in Granville, to whom I have transferred it wholly and unconditionally.
>
> Not an ordinary school mistress, mind you; Miss Frost is not only charming in person, but thoroughly accomplished. I know you will be incredulous; but when I explain the mystery which environs her you will lose your skepticism. Let me tell you, then, in confidence, that last winter, at an artists' reception in New York, I was introduced to a girl whose name I knew as that of an acknowledged queen of society. A little conversation convinced me that she was more than that; that she had a genuine and discriminating love of art; that she despised the frivolous nothings which are dignified as conversations by the butterflies of fashion, and that she regarded life as something more than a succession of parties and receptions. I was strongly attracted; but I learned that she was the possessor of a large fortune, and this precluded the thought of any intimate friendship with her on the part of a penniless artist.
>
> Well, Jack, on the second day after my arrival in Granville, I met this same girl again. Imagine my astonishment at discovering that she was teaching the grammar school in the village, on the splendid stipend of seven dollars a week. Of course she has lost her fortune—how, I have been unable to learn. She is reticent on this subject; but the loss does not seem to affect her spirits. She is

devoting herself earnestly to the work she has chosen, and is succeeding admirably. I declare to you that I yield Miss Frost higher respect now that she is a plain country school teacher than when she was a social leader. That she should give up, uncomplainingly, the gay delights her fortune has procured for her and devote herself to a useful but contracted and perhaps monotonous routine of work, indicates a nobility of nature of which previously I had no assurance.

You will ask to what all this tends. It means, Jack, that I have made up my mind to win her if possible. Between the struggling artist and the wealthy heiress there was a distance too great to be spanned even by love, but now that her estate is on a level with my own I need not hesitate. The same spirit that has enabled her to meet and conquer adversity will sustain her in the self denial and self sacrifice to which she may be called as the wife of a poor man. I have resolved to put my fortune to the test before the close of her school term calls her from Granville. I have some reason to believe that she esteems me, at least. If I am not too precipitate, I hope that esteem may pave the way for a deeper and warmer sentiment. I hope the time may come when I can ask you to congratulate me, as I am sure you will do most heartily, my dear Jack. Ever yours,

Allan Thorpe

P.S.—Lest you should waste your valuable time in exploring back numbers of the newspapers for some mention of Miss Frost in their society gossip, I may as well tell you that this is not her real name. In giving up her fashionable career she has, for a time at least, left behind the name which was associated with it, and taken a new one with the new vocation she has adopted. This might lead to embarrassment; but that will be obviated if she will only consent to accept my name, which has never had any fashionable associations.

P.S.—There is another girl spending the summer here, a Miss Clementina Raymond, of Brooklyn, who assumes airs and graces enough for two. Perhaps it is well that you are not here, for you might be smitten, and she is after higher game. She has "set her cap" for Mr. Randolph Chester, a wealthy bachelor of fifty or more, also a summer resident; but I suspect that he prefers Miss Frost. I do not give myself any trouble on that score. Miss Frost may reject me, but she certainly will not accept Mr. Chester.

CHAPTER ELEVEN

"Theophilus," said Mrs. Wilson, "the flour is out, and we have but half a pound of sugar left."

The minister looked grave.

"My dear," he answered, "it seems to me that something is always out."

"Then," said his wife, smiling faintly, "I suppose you are out of money also."

"I have a dollar and thirty-seven cents in my pocket book, and I do not know when I shall get any more."

"Doesn't the parish owe you something?"

"Yes, but the treasurer told me yesterday, when I spoke to him on the subject, that we must give them time to pay it; that it would create dissatisfaction if I pressed the matter."

"How do they expect us to live?" demanded Mrs. Wilson, as nearly indignant as so meek a woman could be.

"They think we can get along somehow. Besides, the donation party takes place tomorrow. Mr. Stiles told me that I couldn't expect to collect anything till that was over."

"I wish it were over."

"So do I."

"I suppose it will amount to about as much as the others did. People will bring provisions, most of which they will eat themselves. When it is over we'll be the richer by a dozen pincushions, half a dozen pies, a bushel of potatoes, and a few knickknacks for which we have no earthly use."

"I am afraid, my dear, you are getting satirical."

"There is more truth than satire in it, Theophilus, as you know very well. The worst of it is that we are expected to be grateful for what is only an additional burden."

"Well, my dear, you are certainly right; but perhaps we may be more fortunate tomorrow."

At this point Ralph Wilson, the minister's oldest son, came into the room to recite a lesson in the Iliad, and the conversation took a turn.

"I am afraid Ralph will never be able to go to college after all," said his mother.

"I don't see any way at present," said the minister; "but I hope it may be arranged. I wrote last week to my classmate, Professor Ames, of Dartmouth, to inquire what aid Ralph could depend upon from the beneficiary funds."

"Have you had an answer?"

"I received a letter this morning. From what he writes me, I judge that his necessary expenses will be at least four hundred dollars a year——"

"Nearly the amount of your salary."

"And that he can probably procure aid to the amount of two hundred from the beneficiary funds."

"Then it is hopeless. You cannot make up the balance."

"I'm afraid you're right. I think, though, that Ralph should continue his preparation, since, even if he is only prepared to enter, that insures him a good education."

"I might defray a part of my expenses by teaching school in winter," suggested Ralph, who had listened intently to a conversation that so nearly concerned his future.

"You could teach during the junior and senior years," said his father. "I did so myself. During the first two years you would be too young, and it would, besides, be a disadvantage."

Since the donation visit had been decided upon at the sewing circle, it had been a prominent topic of conversation in the village. Though designed to give substantial assistance to the minister's family, it was also to be a festive occasion—a sort of ministerial party—and thus was regarded as a social event.

Fair fingers had been busily at work in the minister's service, and it is safe to say that at least ten pincushions were in the process of manufacture. Chief among the fair workers was Clarissa Bassett, who had a just pride in the superior size and more elaborate workmanship of her pincushions, of which four or five were already on exhibition in the Wilson household.

"I suppose you are going to the donation party, Miss Frost," said Miss Bassett complacently, for she had that morning set the last stitch in what she regarded as the handsomest pincushion she had ever made.

"Yes, I intend to go."

"Have you got your gift ready?" asked Miss Bassett, with natural curiosity.

"I hope to have it ready in time," said Mabel.

"I wish you could see my pincushion," said Clarissa, with subdued enthusiasm. "I think it is the best I ever made."

"Is Mr. Wilson's family in particular need of pincushions?" asked Mabel.

Miss Bassett did not deign to notice the question suggested by Mabel, considering it quite irrelevant.

"I always give pincushions," she said. "People say I have a talent for making them."

Mabel smiled.

"I have no talent at all for that kind of work," she returned. "I should not venture to compete with you. But probably yours will be all that will be required."

"Oh, there are several others who are making them," said Miss Bassett; "but," she added complacently, "I am not afraid to compare mine with any that'll be brought. Old Mrs. Pulsifer showed me hers yesterday—such a looking thing! Made up of odds and ends from her scrap bag. It isn't fit for the kitchen."

"So Mrs. Pulsifer is going to give a pincushion, also?"

"She always does; but if I didn't know how to make one better than she I'd give up altogether."

"Does Mrs. Wilson use a great many pins?" asked Mabel.

Miss Bassett stared.

"I don't know as she uses any more than anybody else," she answered.

"How, then, can she use so many pincushions? Wouldn't some other gift be more acceptable?" Mabel inquired.

"Oh, they'll have other things—cake and pies and such things. It wouldn't be appropriate for me to give anything of that kind."

The next was the eventful day. At four o'clock in the afternoon people began to arrive. The parsonage had just been put in order, and the minister and his wife awaited their visitors.

"Is it necessary for me to be here?" asked Ralph.

"It would hardly look well for you to be away, my son."

"I will stay if you wish it, of course, father; but it always humiliates me. It looks as if we were receiving charity."

"I confess I can't quite rid myself of the same impression," said his father; "but it may be a feeling of worldly pride. We must try to look upon it differently."

"Why can't they give you the value of their presents in money, or by adding to your salary, father?" suggested Ralph.

"They would not be willing. We must accept what they choose to give, and in the form in which they choose to give it."

"I hope, father, I shall some time be able to relieve you from such dependence."

"I wish, for your own sake, you might have the ability, my son, even if I did not require it."

The first to arrive was old Mrs. Pulsifer. She carried in her hand a hideous pincushion, answering the description which Miss Bassett had given of it.

"I made it with my own hands, Mrs. Wilson," she said complacently. "As the apostle says, 'Silver and gold have I none, but such as I have give I unto thee.' "

"Thank you, Mrs. Pulsifer," said the minister's wife, trying to look pleased, and failing.

The next visitor was Mrs. Slocum, who brought a couple of dyspeptic looking pies and a loaf of bread.

"I thought you might need 'em for the company," she said.

"You are very kind, Mrs. Slocum," said Mrs. Wilson. She was quite resigned to the immediate use of Mrs. Slocum's gift.

Next came Mrs. Breck. She, too, contributed some pies and cake, but of a better quality than her predecessor. Close upon her followed Clarissa Bassett, bearing aloft the gorgeous pincushion, which she presented with a complacent flourish to Mrs. Wilson.

"It'll do for your best room, Mrs. Wilson," she said. "I see you've got one pincushion already," eying Mrs. Pulsifer's offering disdainfully.

"I expect several more," said Mrs. Wilson, smiling faintly. "We are generally well remembered in that way."

Next Mrs. and Miss Raymond sailed into the room and made their way to where the minister was.

"Mr. Wilson," said Clementina, with a charming air of patronage, "we do not belong to your flock, but we crave the privilege of participating in this pleasant visit and showing our appreciation of your ministrations. I hope you will accept this small testimonial from my mother and myself."

She left in the minister's hands a bottle of cologne, which she had purchased at the village store that morning for fifty cents.

"Thank you, Miss Raymond," said Mr. Wilson gravely, "quite as much for your words as for your gift."

Was there conscious satire in this speech? If so, neither Miss Raymond nor her mother understood it. They made way for Mr. Randolph Chester, who, indeed, had escorted them to the parsonage.

"Reverend sir," said Mr. Chester with elaborate formality, "I hardly knew what to bring you, but I am sure that books are always welcome to literary men. May I hope that you will give this volume a place in your library?"

As he spoke he handed the minister a small edition of Scott's poems, complete in one volume, and in such fine print as to make it perilous for a person of any except the strongest eyesight to undertake its perusal. Mr. Chester admitted that he was in independent circumstances, and Mr. Wilson had hoped for a present of some real value, but he felt compelled to accept this paltry gift with an appearance of gratitude.

The next half dozen arrivals were laden down with provisions. A committee of ladies took charge of these, and spread a large table, on which all the articles that were cooked were at once placed.

While this was going on, Mrs. Squire Hadley arrived with a dress pattern for Mrs. Wilson. It was a cheap calico of large figure, very repugnant to the taste of the minister's wife, whose heart sank within her as she accepted it, for she knew that Mrs. Hadley would never forgive her if she did not have it made up. Mrs. Hadley had got it at a bargain at the store, where it had lain on the shelves for several seasons without finding a purchaser.

"Dress goods are always acceptable, Mrs. Wilson," she said with the air of one conferring a favor. "I hope you may find this of service."

And Mrs. Wilson was obliged to thank her.

"Brother Wilson," said the Rev. Adoniram Fry in a cheery voice, "I hope I do not intrude. The fact is, I couldn't keep away. I hope you will not be too proud to accept a small gift from your Methodist brother"; and he placed in the minister's hand a five dollar bill.

"Thank you, Brother Fry," said Mr. Wilson, grasping his hand cordially. "I see you understand what I most need"; this last remark being in a lower voice.

"I ought to, Brother Wilson. I never yet knew a minister who couldn't find a use for a five dollar bill."

Deacon Uriah Peabody entered next.

"I've brought you a bushel of apples, parson," he said. "My boy'll carry 'em round to the kitchen. This is a joyful day for you. Your house will overflow with the bounties of Providence."

Such speeches as these the minister, in spite of his meekness, found it hard to listen to without impatience.

"I hope it may," he said gravely. "I shall be glad to have my daily anxieties lightened."

"They will be," said the deacon. "I calc'late you won't to have to buy much for a month to come."

The Rev. Theophilus was better informed. He knew that all but a small remnant of the provisions brought in would be consumed before the company dispersed, and that two days more would suffice to dispose of the last of the donations. But he did not venture to say this. It would have given offense to the visitors, who felt that the minister's family could not be grateful enough for their very liberal gifts.

Mrs. Kent and Mabel were late. The former handed Mr. Wilson an envelope containing a ten dollar bill.

"A joint gift from Miss Frost and myself," she said. "Properly it is not a gift, but a small part of what we owe you."

The minister brightened up, not only because he suspected that the envelope contained money, which was the most acceptable form in which a donation could come, but because the words indicated appreciation, and a proper estimate of his relation to the donation visit. They helped him to bear the patronizing manner of Mrs. Bennett, the butcher's wife, who followed with two cheap collars for Mrs. Wilson.

"Things is brightenin' up for you, Mr. Wilson," said she. "Times is hard, but we're doin' what we can to help you along. I'd like to do more myself, but my husband has so many bad bills, and so much trouble in collectin' his money, that we're straitened when we shouldn't be."

The minister was painfully aware that he was one of the debtors who found it hard to pay his bills, and he knew that Mrs. Bennett's speech was meant for a hint.

Supper was by this time ready, and the ladies and gentlemen filed out to the supper table with alacrity. It was, doubtless, the consciousness that they were engaged in a philanthropic action that increased the appetites of the good people. At any rate, there was very little left on the table when the repast was over. All present seemed in excellent spirits. Congratulations poured in upon the minister and his wife, who, it appeared to be thought, were in great luck.

"Guess this'll put you on your feet, parson," said Deacon Peabody, a little huskily, for he had stuffed half of a large doughnut into his mouth. "The people have come for'ard very liberal today."

"Yes," said the minister unenthusiastically.

"Reminds me of the land flowin' with milk an' honey," resumed the deacon.

"If it could only last," thought Mr. Wilson. On ordinary days there was small appearance of plenty on the minister's frugal board, and, as his guests were consuming about all they brought, there seemed small chance of improvement.

There was a turn in the tide, however. A parcel was brought from the express office, containing a neat cashmere dress, entirely made up, for Mrs. Wilson. This was accompanied by a note from Mary Bridgman, the donor, to this effect:

> Dear Mrs. Wilson:
>
> As I still retain your measure, I have made up this dress for you, and trust it may prove a good fit. I hope you will receive it in the same spirit in which it was sent.
>
> Your true friend,
> Mary Bridgman

It was long since the minister's wife had had a new dress, and the prospect of another had seemed remote enough. Nothing, therefore, could be more timely and acceptable, and the little woman, for the first time during the afternoon, seemed actually cheerful.

"I had no idee Mary was doin' so well," said old Mrs. Slocum. "That cashmere dress must have cost a good deal."

"Mary Bridgman was always extravagant," said Mrs. Hadley disapprovingly. "I don't believe she saves a cent."

Mrs. Hadley may perhaps have felt that the dressmaker's handsome gift was a tacit rebuke for her shabby offering.

Thus far the only gifts of any value had been the dress just mentioned and fifteen dollars in money. It spoke poorly for the liberality of an entire parish, especially when it is considered that three out of the four donors—Mr. Fry, Mary Bridgman and Mabel Frost—were outsiders. Mr. Wilson was not much disappointed. If anything, the visit had been more remunerative than he expected. To one of his scanty income fifteen dollars in cash would be a considerable help. He felt that, on the whole, the donation visit had "paid."

But there was unexpected good fortune in store for him. Ralph came in with a letter from the post-office, postmarked New York.

"I wonder who it can be from, father," he said. "Do you know any one in New York?"

"Only Miss Bridgman, and we have heard from her."

"Better open the letter, parson," said Mrs. Pulsifer, whose curiosity was excited. "We'll all excuse you."

Thus adjured, the minister did so. As he read, his face became luminous with joy, and he fervently ejaculated, "Thank God for all His goodness!"

"What is it, parson?" inquired Deacon Peabody.

"My friends," said the minister, clearing his throat, "I want you all to be partakers of my joy. I will read the letter. It is dated New York.

> "Rev. Mr. Wilson—Dear Sir:
>
> I have this day deposited the sum of five hundred dollars in the Gotham Trust Company of New York city, in your name, and subject to your draft. Pardon me for not communicating my name. Rest assured that it comes from one who appreciates your services, and hopes to be considered your sincere friend and well wisher."

The reading of the letter produced a sensation. Deacon Peabody asked to see it. He put on his spectacles and examined it intently.

"I guess it's genooine," he said cautiously. "Really, Parson Wilson, it makes you a rich man."

"I congratulate you, Mr. Wilson," said Squire Hadley, cordially shaking the minister's hand. "We ain't so liberal as we might be, but I'm glad to find there's somebody that's open handed. Here's ten dollars to add to your five hundred."

"You overwhelm me, Squire Hadley," said the good man. "I feel rebuked for my want of faith in Providence. This morning I awoke with a heavy heart. Little did I dream that the burden was this day to be rolled away. Now I can start fresh, and henceforth I hope to pay my way."

It seemed odd what a sudden accession of respect there was for the minister now that he had money in the bank.

"Oh, Mr. Wilson, don't you be in a hurry about my husband's little account," said Mrs. Bennett. "He'll know you're good for it, and that'll ease his mind."

"Mrs. Bennett," said the minister gravely, "I am obliged for your offer, but I shall attend to your husband's claim at once. I have always wished to pay my debts promptly. Nothing but lack of ability has prevented."

It was quite in order that conjectures should be hazarded as to the unknown donor of this munificent gift. Who was there in New York likely to feel interested in the minister of Granville? Some one suggested that Mr. Randolph Chester lived in New York, and straightway he was questioned on the subject. He smiled, and shrugged his shoulders.

"My dear madam," said he to old Mrs. Pulsifer, "If I am the person I certainly shall not own it. I prefer to remain silent."

This led to the inference that Mr. Chester really gave the money, though no one had suspected him previously of any tendency to liberality. But there were rival claimants. The Raymonds were from Brooklyn, and generally supposed to be wealthy. Could they be Mr. Wilson's unknown friends? When it was suggested to them they replied evasively, neither admitting nor denying it. So opinion was divided, but it was generally thought that it lay between Mr. Chester and the Raymonds. Of course it was not Mary Bridgman, because she sent the handsome dress for Mrs. Wilson.

The minister, however, did not share in the belief. He was quite baffled in his conjecture; but he felt confident that the deposit was not made by the gentleman who had presented him with Scott's poems nor by the giver of the bottle of cheap cologne.

His good fortune was a nine days' wonder, but the mystery remained unsolved. Mr. Wilson went out among his people with a new hope and cheerfulness, and several remarked that he looked ten years younger than before the visit. Life looked brighter to all the little family at the parsonage, and Ralph began to hope that a way might be provided for him to go to college, after all. It is a little odd, too, that now when the minister was comparatively at ease in pecuniary matters, the treasurer of the parish bestirred himself to collect the arrears of his salary, and with such good success that within a week he was able to make Mr. Wilson a payment of seventy-five dollars. So true is it that "Unto him that hath shall be given." So the Rev. Theophilus, who had meditated a journey to New York, to draw upon his newly gained wealth, was able to defer the expedition.

It was a pleasant circumstance that no one appeared to rejoice more sincerely than Adoniram Fry, the Methodist minister, at the good luck of his ministerial brother. Indeed, his hearty friendliness drew the two parishes into more cordial relations, such as surely should exist between Christian people working together for a common purpose.

Meanwhile the summer was passing rapidly, and Mabel's school approached the end of its term. The Granville school closed unusually late in the season. Three years before, an elderly man, who had all his life lived as a bachelor, and, not without reason, had been regarded as a miser, astonished everybody by leaving, in his will, the sum of ten thousand dollars to the town as a fund, the interest to be devoted to lengthening the summer schools. The reason assigned was that in the long summer holidays he had been annoyed by the village children entering his orchard and robbing his fruit, which led him to believe that they would be better off if the vacation were abridged and the school prolonged.

It was near the middle of August, therefore, when Mabel's labors closed. Before the day of examination her experience was marked by two events which call for notice.

Randolph Chester had fully made up his mind to sacrifice his bachelor independence, and wear the fetters of a married man, if Mabel would accept his hand and fortune. That she would do so he did not seriously doubt. He was annoyed by the frequency with which he met Allan Thorpe, but not greatly alarmed.

"A poor artist, like Thorpe, can't marry," he reflected. "Probably he only earns a few hundred dollars a year, and Miss Frost has nothing. Even if he ventured to offer himself she could not seriously hesitate between him and me. I can make her life easy, and, though I am not so young as I once was, I am well preserved."

Mr. Chester surveyed himself in the mirror, and mentally decided that in spite of certain telltale wrinkles about the eyes most persons would not take him for over forty, whereas in reality he would never see fifty again. Do not smile at his delusion. It is a sufficiently common one among people of his age. Indeed, it is natural enough to cling to the semblance of youth. Even philosphers have been known to sigh over the fast coming wrinkles, and express a willingness to resign some of their time earned wisdom for the ruddy bloom of early manhood.

Three days before the school examination Mr. Chester found his opportunity. He called at Mrs. Kent's and found Mabel alone. He felt that the opportunity must be improved.

"I shall attend your examination exercises, Miss Frost," he commenced.

"I shall be glad to see you, Mr. Chester. May I call upon you for a speech?" she added mischievously.

"By no means," said the bachelor hastily. "I am not accustomed to speak on such occasions. Do you intend to leave Granville immediately afterwards?"

"I shall probably remain in the village till the first of September."

"Probably she expects an application to keep the fall term of school," thought Mr. Chester. "I am glad to hear you say so, Miss Frost," he added aloud. "We could hardly spare you."

"Thank you, Mr. Chester. I am afraid you have learned to flatter."

"Indeed I have not, Miss Frost," said Mr. Chester, earnestly. "I may add that I, perhaps, should miss you most of all."

Mabel looked at his face quickly. She suspected what was coming.

"I am certainly obliged to you for your appreciation, Mr. Chester," she returned, without betraying any maidenly confusion.

"It is something more than that," said the bachelor quickly, feeling that the moment had come. "Miss Frost—Mabel—I have learned to love you. I place my hand and my fortune at your feet."

"You are very kind, Mr. Chester, and I am deeply indebted to you for the compliment you have paid me; but I cannot marry without love, and I do not love you."

"It will come in time," urged Mr. Chester. "All I ask is that you marry me, and I will take the risk of that."

"But I cannot," said Mabel. "We should find too late that we had made a mistake."

In spite of his love, Randolph Chester felt a little irritated at Mabel's indifference to her own interests.

"I am afraid, Miss Frost," he said, "you don't understand how much I offer you. I possess independent means. I can release you from the slavery of the schoolroom, and provide for you a life of ease. We will live in the city during the greater part of the year, and in the summer come to Granville, or any other place you would prefer. It is not an unpleasant life I offer you."

"I don't think we take the same view of marriage, Mr. Chester," said Mabel. "I should not be willing to marry in order to live at ease, or to escape the 'slavery of the schoolroom,' which I have found pleasant. I thank you for the compliment you have paid me, but it is impossible."

She spoke decisively, and Mr. Chester could not escape the conviction that his answer was final. He was not overwhelmed with grief, but he was bitterly angry.

"Of course you can do as you please, Miss Frost," he said sharply.

"I hope you won't find out your mistake when it is too late. If you think of marrying that artist fellow, Thorpe, I may as well tell you that he can hardly support himself, much less a wife."

This was more than Mabel could bear. She rose to her feet, and her eyes flashed fire.

"You have no right to say this," she exclaimed. "Mr. Thorpe has never spoken to me of love. As for his circumstances, I have never considered them. I only know that *he* is a gentleman."

She swept out of the room indignantly, leaving Mr. Chester rather bewildered. He took his hat and left the house, sorely disappointed, and still more angry. His vanity had received a severe wound, which would take a longer time to heal than his heart, which had not been so seriously affected.

As he walked towards the hotel he felt very bitter towards Mabel, and scowled fiercely at Allan Thorpe, whom he happened to meet on the way, though, as it was dark, the artist was happily unconscious of it. He thirsted for revenge. He wished to show Mabel that he was not inconsolable. Unhappily for the bachelor, he was in this mood when he reached the hotel and met Miss Clementina Raymond. He did not care a particle for her, but spite against Miss Frost hurried him on to the avowal of a passion that he did not feel. His offer was rather a cool, business-like proposal than an impulsive declaration of affection. But Clementina made up for his lack of sentiment by a bashful confusion, which was very well assumed.

"I am *so* surprised, and *so* embarrassed, Mr. Chester," she said. "How could I dream that you were kind enough to regard me with such sentiments? I ought, perhaps, to consult mamma."

"If you have any doubt about your answer," said Mr. Chester abruptly, already half regretting his precipitancy, "say so without hesitation."

Evidently the delay would be dangerous, and Clementina decided to settle the matter at once.

"No," she said, "I will not consult mamma. I know her high opinion of you, dear Mr. Chester—let me say Randolph. If you care for this little hand, it is yours," and she timidly laid a large and well developed palm in his. She was rather disappointed that he did not press it to his lips. In all the novels she had taken from the Brooklyn Mercantile Library, that was what enraptured lovers always did when accepted. Mr. Chester just pressed the hand slightly, and, rising, said in a business-like way; "Very well, Miss Raymond, we will consider the matter settled. I will leave you now, as you will probably wish to tell your mother."

This was the way in which Clementina told her mother the news:——

"Mamma, that old goose has proposed, and I have accepted him."

"What old goose?"

"Randolph Chester, of course. He's as old as the hills, but he's got money."

"And you are nearly twenty-five, my love."

"Oh, bother, mamma! What's the use of mentioning my age? Somebody might be within hearing. Remember, if he asks how old I am, you are not to answer so impertinent a question."

"Very well, Clementina. Of course, my child, our interests are the same. I am really glad you will have a husband of means. It has been very hard to keep up a genteel appearance on our limited income, and it will be a relief to have some one to provide."

"You are right, mother. Of course I wouldn't think of marrying the old mummy if he hadn't plenty of money. He thinks we are rich; so you must be careful not to drop any hint of our real situation until after we are married. I wonder if I can't induce him to take me to Europe for our wedding tour."

"That would be a very pleasant arrangement, Clementina. I always wanted to go to Europe."

"Of course you couldn't go, mamma," said the selfish daughter. "I am sure Mr. Chester wouldn't agree to it. I may find it very hard to induce him to take me."

"I should be very lonely if you left me at home," said the disappointed mother.

"I should write you often. That would do almost as well."

Mrs. Raymond did not think so, but she knew her daughter's hard, ingrained selfishness too well to press the matter. She received Mr. Chester on the footing of a son-in-law most graciously, though it did occur to her that it would have been better if *she* could have secured him as a husband instead of Clementina; then she could have made the European tour.

It may be as well, however, to say here that neither to mother nor daughter were revealed the scenic charms of Europe. When Randolph

Chester discovered that he had married a genteel pauper he was deeply incensed, and was in no mood to grant favors to the wife who had deceived him. He married in haste, to repent at leisure.

CHAPTER TWELVE

The day of examination came, and the small schoolroom was thronged with visitors. The exercises passed off in the most satisfactory manner. Squire Hadley, as chairman of the School Committee, made the first speech. It was not a model of eloquence, but he made it clear that he considered the school a success and took credit to himself for engaging so competent a teacher. Mr. Wilson followed. He, too, expressed hearty approval of the exercises, and tendered his cordial congratulations to Miss Frost for remarkable success in inspiring the scholars with a love of learning.

He hoped the town would be able to retain the services of so accomplished an instructress. To him succeeded Adoniram Fry, who, in a jocular way, lamented that as a boy it had not been in his power to be a scholar under Miss Frost's instruction. All were complimentary, and Mabel's cheeks were flushed with pleasure.

Randolph Chester was not present at the closing exercises. Neither were the Raymonds. The engagement had leaked out, and therefore their absence did not excite surprise. It was ascertained that they had driven to a neighboring town. It was not discovered, however, till later, what their errand was. They drove at once to the residence of a clergyman, and when they returned Clementina was Mrs. Randolph Chester. Clementina herself had artfully hinted how romantic it would be, and how people would be taken by surprise. Mr. Chester cared nothing for this; but it occurred to him that Mabel would be mortified on learning how quickly he had been consoled for her loss. Poor Mr. Chester! In after years he looked upon this as the most idiotic act of his life.

In the evening Allan Thorpe called and invited Mabel to go out for a walk. It was a beautiful moonlit night. They walked slowly to the pond, which was not far away, and sat down on a rustic seat beneath a wide spreading oak. They had been talking on various things for some time, when a sudden silence came upon both. It was at length broken by the young artist.

"I hope you will forgive me for bringing you here," he said.

"Why should you want forgiveness?" she asked, very much surprised.

"Because I brought you here with a special object in view. Rebuke me if you will, but—Mabel, I love you."

She did not seem much surprised.

"How long has it been so?" she asked in a low voice.

"I began to love you," he answered, "when I first saw you at the artists' reception. But you were so far removed from me that I did not dare to avow it, even to myself. You were a rich social queen, and I was a poor man. I should never have dared to tell you all this if you had not lost your wealth."

"Does this make me any more worthy?" asked Mabel smiling.

"It has brought you nearer to me. When I saw how bravely you met adverse fortune; when I saw a girl brought up to every luxury, as you were, quietly devoting herself to teaching a village school, I rejoiced. I admired you more than ever, and I resolved to win you if possible. Can you give me a hope, Mabel?"

He bent over her with a look of tender affection in his manly face.

"I won't keep you in suspense, Allan," she said with an answering look. "I have not known you long, but long enough to trust my future in your hands."

After a while Allan Thorpe began to discuss his plans and hopes for the future.

"I am beginning to be successful," he said. "I can, even now, support you in a modest way, and with health I feel assured of a larger—I hope a much larger—income in time. I can relieve you from teaching at once."

Mabel smiled.

"But suppose I do not consider it a burden. Suppose I like it."

"Then you can teach me."

"It might become monotonous to have only one pupil."

"I hope not," said Allan earnestly.

When he pressed her to name an early day for their marriage, Mabel said: "Before we go any further, I have a confession to make. I hope it won't be disagreeable to you."

He silently inclined his head to listen.

"Who told you I had lost my property?" she asked.

"No one. I inferred it from finding you here, teaching a village school for seven dollars a week," replied Allan.

"What! Have you inquired my income so exactly? I fear you are mercenary."

"I can remember the time—not so long since, either—when I earned less than that by my art. But, Mabel, what do you mean by your questions? Of course you have lost your property."

"Then my banker has failed to inform me of it. No, Allan, I am no poorer than I ever was."

"Why, then, did you become a teacher?" asked Allan Thorpe, bewildered.

"Because I wished to be of some service to my kind; because I was tired of the hollow frivolity of the fashionable world. I don't regret my experiment. I never expected to be so richly rewarded."

"And you, as rich as ever, bestow your hand on a poor artist?" he exclaimed almost incredulously.

"Unless the poor artist withdraws his offer," she answered with a smile.

Of the conversation that followed it is needful only to report that it was mutually decided that Mabel's secret was to be kept for the present. She was still to be the poor school teacher in the eyes of Granville. The marriage was to take place in October, Mabel being reconciled to the briefness of the engagement by the representation that October would be a favorable month for a voyage to Europe. They had already decided to spend two years in Italy. Mabel had always longed to see Italy, and it would no doubt be full of delightful opportunities of improvement in his art for Allan Thorpe.

Mabel's engagement made a second sensation, Mr. Chester's elopement being the first. Many were the congratulations offered, though these were mingled with regret that so good a teacher should be lost to the village. Mr. Chester heard the news in gloomy silence. His wife remarked patronizingly that it was a very suitable match, for "both are as poor as poverty, goodness knows!"

The wedding took place quietly in October, and in Granville. No one as yet knew that Mabel was other than she seemed, though Mr. Wilson had been informed of her real name. When, however, a check for five hundred dollars was handed to him as his fee for celebrating the marriage, he faltered in amazement, as he inquired, "What does this mean, Allan?"

"It means, my dear uncle, that Mabel is not only rich in every virtue and every accomplishment, but she is also burdened with a large portion of this world's goods. This is my first opportunity for saying what she authorized me to say, that we will gladly defray Ralph's expenses through college whenever you are ready to send him."

"God is indeed good to me and mine!" said the minister, his face beaming with happiness. "My dear child"—this was to Mabel—"may you always be as happy as you have made us."

"You have made us all happy, dear Mabel," said her husband. "It was indeed a blessed day when you came to Granville to teach."

THE DISAGREEABLE WOMAN
A SOCIAL MYSTERY

THE DISAGREEABLE WOMAN
A SOCIAL MYSTERY

To My Readers

In reading Miss Beatrice Harraden's charming idyl "Ships That Pass in the Night," it occurred to me that if there were Disagreeable Men there are also Disagreeable Women. Hence this story.

CHAPTER ONE
A SOCIAL MYSTERY

"If I live till next July, I shall be twenty-nine years old," simpered the young widow, and she looked around the table, as if to note the effect of such an incredible statement.

"You look much older," said the Disagreeable Woman, looking up from her tea and buttered toast.

There was a general silence, and the boarders noted with curiosity the effect of this somewhat unceremonious remark.

Mrs. Wyman, the young widow, flushed and directed an angry and scornful look at the last speaker.

"I am sure I am very much obliged to you," she said.

"You are quite welcome," said the Disagreeable Woman, calmly.

"You look older than I do," said the widow, sharply.

"Very possibly," said the Disagreeable Woman, not at all excited.

"Do you mind telling us how old you are?"

"Not at all! I have reached the age——"

All bent forward to listen. Why is it that we take so much interest in the ages of our acquaintances? There was evidently a strong desire to learn the age of the Disagreeable Woman. But she disappointed the general expectation.

"I have reached the age of discretion," she continued, finishing the sentence.

"Who is that woman?" I asked my next neighbor, for I was a newcomer at Mrs. Gray's table.

"Wait till after breakfast and I will tell you," he answered.

Mrs. Gray kept a large boarding-house on Waverly Place. Some fifteen boarders were gathered about the large table. I may have occasion to refer to some of them later. But first I will speak of myself.

I was a young medical practitioner, who after practicing for a year in a Jersey village had come to New York in quest of a metropolitan practice and reputation. I was not quite penniless, having five hundred dollars left over from the legacy of an old aunt, the rest of which had been used to defray the expenses of my education. I had not yet come to realize how small a sum this was for a professional start in the city. I had hired an office, provided with a cabinet bedstead, and thus saved room rent. For table board I had been referred to Mrs. Gray's boarding-house, on Waverly Place.

"I boarded there once," said the friend who recommended me, "and found not only a fair table but a very social and entertaining family of boarders. They were of all classes," he continued, "from literateurs to dry goods clerks, schoolteachers, actors, and broken-down professionals."

This description piqued my curiosity, and I enrolled myself as one of Mrs. Gray's boarders, finding her terms not beyond my modest means.

But in his list of boarders he forgot—the Disagreeable Woman, who must have come after his departure.

She was tall, inclined to be slender, with a keen face and singular eyes. She never seemed to be excited, but was always calm and self-possessed. She seemed to have keen insight into character, and as may already be inferred, of remarkable and even perhaps rude plainness of speech. Yet though she said sharp things she never seemed actuated by malice or ill-nature. She did not converse much, but was always ready to rebuke pretension and humbug as in the case of the young widow. What she said of her was quite correct. I judged from her appearance that Mrs. Wyman must be at least thirty-five years old, and possibly more. She evidently did not intend to remain a widow longer than was absolutely necessary.

She paid attention to every male boarder at the table, neglecting none. She even made overtures to Prof. Poppendorf, a learned German, with a deep bass voice and a German accent, whose green goggles and shaggy hair, somewhat grizzled, made him a picturesque personality.

We all enjoyed the rebuff which Mrs. Wyman received from the Disagreeable Woman, though it made us slightly afraid of her lest our turns might come next.

But I am keeping my readers from my friend's promised account of the lady who had excited my curiosity.

CHAPTER TWO
THE MYSTERY DEEPENS

"The first time I met the Disagreeable Woman," said my neighbor, who was a commercial traveler, "was on my return from a business trip. Looking about the table to see what changes had occurred in the family, I saw sitting opposite to me a woman of somewhat unusual appearance, whose caustic speech made her feared by the rest of the boarders. This was three months since."

"What is her name?" I asked.

"Upon my word," he answered reflectively, "I am so accustomed to hear her spoken of as the Disagreeable Woman that I hardly remember. Let me see—yes, it is Blagden."

"And the first name?"

"Jane."

"Is it Miss or Mrs. Blagden?"

"I don't know."

"She has been here three months and you do not know," I said, in surprise.

"Precisely."

"Did it never occur to any one to ask her?"

"Yes, Mrs. Wyman asked her one day."

"And what did she reply?"

"Whichever you please—it is quite immaterial."

"Do you think she has any reason to maintain secrecy on this point?"

"I think not. She probably takes the ground that it is nobody's business but her own."

"How soon did she obtain her designation of the 'Disagreeable Woman?' "

"Almost immediately I judge. When I first met her she had been a member of Mrs. Gray's household for a week, and already this was the way she was spoken of."

"I suppose she does not live in the house?"

"No."

"Where then?"

"No one knows. She comes to her meals punctually, turning into Waverly Place from Broadway."

"Has no one ever thought of following her home?"

"Yes. A young broker's clerk, on a wager, attempted to track her to her lodging place. She was sharp enough to detect his purpose. When they reached Broadway she turned suddenly and confronted him. 'Are you going up or down Broadway?' she asked. 'Up Broadway,' he answered with some hesitation, 'Then good evening! I go in the opposite direction.' Of course there was nothing for him to do but to accept the hint, which was certainly pointed enough."

"She must be a woman with a history," I said, thoughtfully.

"Most women have histories."

"But not out of the common."

"True. What now do you conjecture as to Miss Blagden's history?"

"I am utterly at a loss."

"Do you think she has had a disappointment?"

"She does not look impressionable. One cannot conceive of her as having an affair of the heart."

"Do you think she has any employment?"

"If so, no one has been able to conjecture what it is."

"I don't know. One cannot always judge by the exterior."

"To me she seems like an advocate of Woman's Rights, perhaps a lecturer on that subject."

"Possibly, but I know of nothing to throw light on her business or her views."

"Do you think she is a woman of means?"

"Ah," said my friend, smiling, "you are really beginning to show interest in her. I believe you are unmarried?"

The suggestion was grotesque and I could not help smiling.

"I should pity the man who married the 'Disagreeable Woman,' " I made answer.

"I don't know. She is not beautiful, certainly, nor attractive, but I don't think she is as ill-natured as she appears."

"Is this conjecture on your part?"

"Not wholly. Did you notice the young woman who sat on her left?"

"Yes."

"We know her as the young woman from Macy's. Well, a month since she was sick for a week, and unable to pay her board. She occupies a hall bedroom on the upper floor. Miss Blagden guessed her trouble, and as she left the table on Saturday night put into her hands an envelope without a word. When it was opened it proved to contain ten dollars, sufficient to pay two weeks' board."

"Come, there seems to be something human about the Disagreeable Woman."

"Just so. To us it was a revelation. But she would not allow herself to be thanked."

"That last piece of information interests me. My office practice at present is very limited, and I find my small capital going fast. I may need the good office of Miss Blagden."

"I hope not, but I must leave you. My employers have sent me an orchestra ticket to Palmer's theatre."

"I hope you will enjoy yourself."

So we parted company. I went to my office, and spent a part of the evening in searching among my medical books for some light on a case that had baffled me. But from time to time my attention was distracted by thoughts of the Disagreeable Woman.

CHAPTER THREE
PROF. POPPENDORF

Dinner was nearly over. The dessert had been succeeded by a dish of withered russet apples, when Mrs. Gray, leaning forward a little, said: "If the boarders will kindly remain a short time, Prof. Poppendorf has an interesting communication to make.

The learned professor cleared his throat, removed his goggles for an instant, and after wiping them carefully with a red silk handkerchief, replaced them on a nose of large proportions.

"My friends," he said, "on Thursday next I am to deliver a lecture at Schiller Hall, on Second Avenue, and I hope I may have the honor of seeing you all present. The tickets are fifty cents."

"May I ask the subject of your lecture, Professor?" asked Mrs. Wyman, with an appearance of interest.

"I shall lecture on 'The Material and the Immaterial,' " answered the Professor, in a deep bass voice.

The boarders looked puzzled. The announcement of the subject did not seem to excite interest.

"Shall you treat the subject in a popular manner, Prof. Poppendorf?" asked the Disagreeable Woman, in a tone that did not necessarily suggest sarcasm.

Prof. Poppendorf seemed puzzled.

"I do not know!" he answered, "if it will be popular—I hope it will be instructive."

"Will there be any jokes in it, Professor?" asked Sam Lindsay, a vocalist from an uptown Dime Museum.

"Jokes!" repeated the Professor, evidently scandalized. "It would not be appropriate. The subject is metaphysical. If you want jokes you must go to the variety theatre."

"True," said Lindsay, "or to the Dime Museums. We've got a man at our place who will make you split your sides laughing."

"I have here some tickets," continued the Professor, "some tickets which I shall be glad to dispose of in advance," and he drew out a package of perhaps twenty-five. "Miss Blagden, I hope you will patronize me."

"You may give me two," said the Disagreeable Woman, drawing a dollar bill from her pocket, and passing it to the Professor.

"You take two tickets?" said Mrs. Wyman, with a knowing smile. "I suppose there is a gentleman in the case."

"You are mistaken," said the Disagreeable Woman, quietly.

"You don't want both tickets for yourself, surely?"

"No, I shall use neither of them."

"You will give them away, then?"

"I do not think so."

"Why, then——"

"Why then do I buy them? Out of compliment to our friend, Prof. Poppendorf, who, I hope, will win a success."

"I thank you," said the Professor, "but I should be glad to have you honor my lecture with your presence."

"I feel no particular interest in 'The Material and the Immaterial,'" said Mrs. Blagden. "Besides I am not sure whether I should get any clearer ideas respecting them from attending your lecture."

"You do not flatter the Professor," said Mrs. Wyman, appearing shocked.

"No, I never flatter any one. Why should I?" returned the Disagreeable Woman.

"I like to be flattered," said the widow, simpering. "I like to be told that I am young and charming."

"Even if you are not."

Mrs. Wyman colored, and looked annoyed. She evidently did not care to continue her conversation with the Disagreeable Woman.

"Professor Poppendorf," she said, "will you allow me to suggest something which will enable you to sell a good many tickets?"

"I should be very glad to hear," said the Professor, eagerly.

"Get Chauncey M. Depew to preside, and introduce you to the audience."

"I did ask him, but he could not come. He is engaged to preside at a dinner given to the Yale Football Team."

"Does Mr. Depew kick football?" asked the young woman from Macy's.

"I think not," I ventured to say. "Gentlemen over forty seldom indulge in athletics."

"I am so sorry you can't get Mr. Depew," said Mrs. Wyman. "I should so like to hear him."

"You will hear *me,*" said Prof. Poppendorf, with dignity, "if you will kindly buy a ticket."

Mrs. Wyman looked embarrassed. She had a fair income, but carried economy to a fine point.

"Perhaps," she said, with a hesitating glance at the person of whom she spoke, "Miss Blagden will give me one of her tickets, as she does not intend to use either."

"That wouldn't help the professor," said Miss Blagden, quietly. "You had better buy one of him."

The Professor evidently approved this suggestion.

Mrs. Wyman reluctantly drew from her pocket forty-five cents in change, and tendered it to the Professor.

"I will owe you a nickel," she said.

"You can pay it any time, my dear lady," said the Professor, politely, as he passed a ticket to the widow.

Nearly all at the table took tickets, but the young woman from Macy's was not of the number. The price was small, but she needed gloves, and could not spare even fifty cents.

"Prof. Poppendorf," said a young man, who was attached as a reporter to one of the great morning dailies, "did I not hear you say once that you knew Bismarck?"

"Ah! yes," said the Professor, "I was at the University with Bismarck."

"How nice!" said Mrs. Wyman, with girlish enthusiasm. "It must have been a great privilege."

"I don't know," said Prof. Poppendorf, deliberately. "Bismarck was not a great student. He would not study. Bismarck was wild."

"Did he drink beer?" asked the widow.

"Of course," answered the Professor, surprised; "why should he not? I drank beer myself."

"Is it possible? I would not have believed it. Fie, Professor!"

"Beer is a very good thing" said the Professor, gravely. "There were not many of the students who could drink as much as Bismarck."

"And did Bismarck care for young ladies?"

"I should think so. I had a duel with Bismarck myself about a young *mädchen.*"

More than one of the boarders smiled. It was so difficult to associate the gray old Professor with anything that savored of gallantry.

"Oh, yes," he continued, "Bismarck was the devil among the girls."

"Oh, Professor, I am shocked! You should not use such a word as devil at the table."

"What, then, do you call him?" asked Prof. Poppendorf.

"He is not mentioned in polite society. But tell us about the duel—were you wounded?"

"You see that scar," said the Professor, pointing to a slight disfigurement of his left cheek. "That was given me by Bismarck."

"Oh, how interesting! It is almost like seeing Bismarck himself."

"Prof. Poppendorf," said the Disagreeable Woman, "why do you not lecture on Bismarck, instead of the dry subject you have announced?"

"You admire Bismarck, then, my dear lady?"

"Not at all."

"But I don't understand."

"The people are interested in him. They don't care for the 'Material and the Immaterial.'"

"That is a good suggestion, Professor," said the widow. "I would much rather hear about Bismarck. *I* admire him. Why do you not, Miss Blagden?"

"Because he was a second-hand autocrat," said the Disagreeable Woman.

"Again I do not understand," said the Professor.

"He was the servant of the Emperor. His authority did not come from the people."

There was some further conversation, and Prof. Poppendorf promised that his next lecture should be upon Bismarck.

CHAPTER FOUR
PROF. POPPENDORF'S LECTURE

We all sat at supper on Thursday evening. There was a general air of expectation. It was on this evening that Prof. Poppendorf was to give his lecture. We all gazed at him with more than ordinary interest. The old Professor, gray and grim-visaged, sat more than usually erect, and his manner and bearing were marked by unusual dignity. He felt himself to be the hero of the hour.

I have neglected to say that Mrs. Wyman had been transferred to the seat adjoining mine. As she could not do without masculine attention I suspect that this arrangement was prompted by herself. Henceforth I was favored with the greater part of her conversation.

"I am quite looking forward to Prof. Poppendorf's lecture!" she said. "You are going, are you not?"

"I think so, but I can't say I am looking forward to it. I fancy it will be dry and difficult to understand."

"You think he is a learned man, do you not?"

"Very probably—in certain directions."

"Dr. Fenwick, I am going to ask a favor of you."

"I hope it isn't money," thought I, for I was beginning to have some anxiety about my steadily dwindling bank account.

"Name it, Mrs. Wyman," I said, somewhat nervously.

"I am almost ashamed to say it, but I don't like to go to the lecture alone. Would you mind giving me your escort?"

"With pleasure," I answered.

"My answer was not quite truthful, for I had intended to ask the young woman from Macy's to accompany me. She was no intellectual, but she had a fresh country face and complexion; she came from Pomfret, Connecticut, and was at least ten years younger than Mrs. Wyman. But what could I say? I had not the moral courage to refuse a lady.

"Thank you very much. Now I shall look forward to the evening with pleasure."

"You are complimentary. Do you expect to understand the lecture?"

"I don't know. I never gave much thought to the 'Material and Immaterial.'"

"Possibly we may understand as much about the subject as the Professor himself."

"Oh, how severe you are! Now I have great faith in the Professor's learning."

"He ought to be learned. He certainly has no physical beauty."

Mrs. Wyman laughed.

"I suppose few learned men are handsome," she said.

"Then perhaps I may console myself for having so little learning. Do you think the same rule holds good with ladies?"

"To a certain extent. I am sure the principal of the seminary I attended was frightfully plain; but I am sure she was learned. Prof. Poppendorf, have you sold many lecture tickets?"

"Quite a few!" answered the Professor, vaguely.

"Are you going to attend the lecture, Miss Blagden?" asked the widow.

"Miss Canby and I have agreed to go together."

Miss Canby was the young woman from Macy's. The Disagreeable Woman, finding that she wished to attend the lecture, offered her a ticket and her company, both being thankfully accepted. So that after all my escort was not needed by the young woman, and I lost nothing by my attention to the widow.

We did not rise from the table till seven o'clock. Mrs. Wyman excused herself for a short time. She wished to dress for the lecture. The gentlemen withdrew to the reception room, a small and very narrow room on one side of the hall, and waited for the ladies to appear. Among those who seated themselves there was the Disagreeable Woman. She waited for the appearance of the young woman from Macy's, whom she was to accompany to the lecture. Somehow she did not seem out of place in the assemblage of men.

"You did not at first propose to hear Prof. Poppendorf?" I remarked.

"No; I shall not enjoy it. But I found Miss Canby wished to attend."

"We shall probably know a good deal more about the Material and the Immaterial when we return."

"Possibly we shall know as much as the Professor himself," she answered, quietly.

"I am afraid you are no hero worshiper, Miss Blagden."

"Do you refer to the Professor as a hero?"

"He is the hero of this evening."

"Perhaps so. We will see."

Prof. Poppendorf looked into the reception room previous to leaving the house. He wore a long coat, or surtout, as it used to be called—tightly buttoned around his spare figure. There was a rose in his buttonhole. I had never seen one there before, but then this was a special occasion. He seemed in good spirits, as one on the eve of a triumph. He was content with one comprehensive glance. Then he opened the front door, and went out.

Just then Mrs. Wyman tripped into the room, closely followed by Ruth Canby. The widow was quite radiant. I can't undertake to itemize her splendor. She looked like a social butterfly.

Quite in contrast with her was the young woman from Macy's, whose garb was almost Quaker-like in its simplicity. Mrs. Wyman surveyed her with a contemptuous glance, and no doubt mentally contrasted her plainness with her own showy apparel. But the Disagreeable Woman's eye seemed to rest approvingly on her young companion. They started out ahead of the rest of us.

"What a very plain person Miss Canby is!" said the widow, as we emerged into the street, her arm resting lightly in mine.

"Do you refer to her dress or her face and figure?"

"Well, to both."

"She dresses plainly; but I suspect that is dictated by economy. She has a pleasant face."

"It is the face of a peasant."

"I didn't know there were any peasants in America."

"Well, you understand what I mean. She looks like a country girl."

"Perhaps so, but is that an objection?"

"Few country girls are stylish."

"I don't myself care so much for style as for good health and a good heart."

"Really, Dr. Fenwick, your ideas are very old-fashioned. In that respect you resemble my dear, departed husband."

"Is it permitted to ask whether your husband has long been dead?"

"I have been a widow six years," said Mrs. Wyman, with an ostentatious sigh. "I was quite a girl when my dear husband died."

According to her own chronology, she was twenty-three. In all probability she became a widow at twenty-nine or thirty. But of course I could not insinuate any doubt of a lady's word.

"And you have never been tempted to marry again?" I essayed with great lack of prudence.

"Oh, Dr. Fenwick, do you think it would be right?" said the widow, leaning more heavily on my arm.

"If you should meet one who was congenial to you. I don't know why not."

"I have always thought that if I ever married again I would select a professional gentleman," murmured the widow.

I began to understand my danger and tried a diversion.

"I don't know if you would consider Prof. Poppendorf a professional gentleman," I said.

"Oh, how horrid! Who would marry such an old fossil?"

"It is well that the Professor does not hear you."

Perhaps this conversation is hardly worth recording, but it throws some light on the character of the widow. Moreover it satisfied me that should I desire to marry her there would be no violent opposition on her part. But, truth to tell, I would have preferred the young woman from Macy's, despite the criticism of Mrs. Wyman. One was artificial, the other was natural.

We reached Schiller Hall, after a long walk. It was a small hall, looking something like a college recitation room.

Prof. Poppendorf took his place behind a desk on the platform and looked about him. There were scarcely a hundred persons, all told, in the audience. The men, as a general thing, were shabbily dressed, and elderly. There were perhaps twenty women, with whom dress was a secondary consideration.

"Did you ever see such frights, doctor?" whispered the widow.

"You are the only stylishly dressed woman in the hall."

Mrs. Wyman looked gratified.

The Professor commenced a long and rather incomprehensible talk, in which the words material and immaterial occurred at frequent intervals. There may have been some in the audience who understood him, but I was not one of them.

"Do you understand him?" I asked the widow.

"Not wholly," she answered, guardedly.

I was forced to smile, for she looked quite bewildered.

The Professor closed thus: "Thus you will see, my friends, that much that we call material is immaterial, while *per contra,* that which is usually called immaterial is material."

"A very satisfactory conclusion," I remarked, turning to the widow.

"Quite so," she answered, vaguely.

"I thank you for your attention, my friends," said the Professor, with a bow.

There was faint applause, in which I assisted.

The Professor looked gratified, and we all rose and quietly left the hall. I walked out behind Miss Canby and the Disagreeable Woman.

"How did you like the lecture, Miss Blagden?" I inquired.

"Probably as much as you did," she answered, dryly.

"What do you think of the Professor, now?"

"He seems to know a good deal that isn't worth knowing."

CHAPTER FIVE
A CONVERSATION WITH THE DISAGREEABLE WOMAN

One afternoon between five and six o'clock I was passing the Star Theatre, when I overtook the Disagreeable Woman.

I had only exchanged a few remarks with her at the table, and scarcely felt acquainted. I greeted her, however, and waited with some curiosity to see what she would have to say to me.

"Dr. Fenwick, I believe?" she said.

"Yes; are you on your way to supper?"

"I am. Have you had a busy day?"

As she said this she looked at me sharply.

"I have had two patients, Miss Blagden. I am a young physician, and not well known yet. I advance slowly."

"You have practiced in the country?"

"Yes."

"Pardon me, but would it not have been better to remain there, where you were known, than to come to a large city where you are as one of the sands of the sea?"

"I sometimes ask myself that question, but as yet I am unprepared with an answer. I am ambitious, and the city offers a much larger field."

"With a plenty of laborers already here."

"Yes."

"I suppose you have confidence in yourself?"

Again she eyed me sharply.

"Yes and no. I have a fair professional training, and this gives me some confidence. But sometimes, it would be greater if I had an extensive practice, I feel baffled, and shrink from the responsibility that a physician always assumes."

"I am glad to hear you say so," she remarked, approvingly. Modesty is becoming in any profession. Do you feel encouraged by your success thus far?"

"I am gaining, but my progress seems slow. I have not yet reached the point when I am self-supporting."

She looked at me thoughtfully.

"Of course you would not have established yourself here if you had not a reserve fund to fall back upon? But perhaps I am showing too much curiosity."

"No, I do not regard it as curiosity, only as a kind interest in my welfare."

"You judge me right."

"I brought with me a few hundred dollars, Miss Blagden—what was left to me from the legacy of a good aunt—but I have already used a quarter of it, and every month it grows less."

"I feel an interest in young men—I am free to say this without any fear of being misunderstood, being an old woman——"

"An old woman?"

"Well, I am more than twenty-nine."

We both smiled, for this was the age that Mrs. Wyman owned up to.

"At any rate," she resumed, "I am considerably older than you. I will admit, Dr. Fenwick, that I am not a blind believer in the medical profession. There are some, even of those who have achieved a certain measure of success, whom I look upon as solemn pretenders."

"Yet if you were quite ill you would call in a physician?"

"Yes. I am not quite foolish enough undertake to doctor myself in a serious illness. But I would repose unquestioning faith in no one, however eminent."

"I don't think we shall disagree on that point. A physician understands his own limitations better than any outsider."

"Come, I think you will do," she said, pleasantly. "If I am ill at any time I shall probably call you in."

"Thank you."

"And I should criticize your treatment. If you gave me any bread pills, I should probably detect the imposture."

"I should prefer, as a patient, bread pills to many that are prescribed."

"You seem to to be a sensible man, Dr. Fenwick. I shall hope to have other opportunities of conversing with you. Let me know from time to time how you are succeeding."

"Thank you. I am glad you are sufficiently interested in me to make the request."

By this time we had reached the boarding-house. We could see Mrs. Wyman at the window of the reception room. She was evidently surprised and amused to see us together. I was sure that I should hear more of it, and I was not mistaken.

"Oh, Dr. Fenwick," she said playfully, as she took a seat beside me at the table. "I caught you that time."

"I don't understand you," I said, innocently.

"Oh, yes, you do. Didn't I see you and Miss Blagden coming in together?"

"Yes."

"I thought you would confess. Did you have a pleasant walk?"

"It was only from the Star Theatre."

"I see you are beginning to apologize. You could say a good deal between Waverly Place and the Star Theatre."

"We did."

"So I thought. I suppose you were discussing your fellow boarders, including poor me."

"Not at all."

"Then my name was not mentioned?"

"Yes, I believe you were referred to."

"What did she say about me?" inquired the widow, eagerly.

"Only that she was older than you."

"Mercy, I should think she was. Why, she's forty if she's a day. Don't you think so?"

"I am no judge of ladies' ages."

"I am glad you are not. Not that I am sensitive about my own. I am perfectly willing to own that I am twenty-seven."

"I thought you said twenty-nine, the other evening?"

"True, I am twenty-nine, but I said twenty-seven to see if you would remember. I suppose gentlemen are never sensitive about their ages."

"I don't know. I am twenty-six, and wish I were thirty-six."

"Mercy, what a strange wish! How can you possibly wish that you were older."

"Because I could make a larger income. It is all very well to be a young minister, but a young doctor does not inspire confidence."

"I am sure I would rather call in a young doctor unless I were *very* sick."

"There it is! Unless you were very sick."

"But even then," said the widow, coquettishly, "I am sure I should feel confidence in you, Dr. Fenwick. You wouldn't prescribe very nasty pills, would you?"

"I would order bread pills, if I thought they would answer the purpose."

"That would be nice. But you haven't answered my question. What were you and Miss Blagden talking about?"

"About doctors; she hasn't much faith in men of my profession."

"Or of any other, I fancy. What do you think of her?"

"That is a leading question, Mrs. Wyman; I haven't thought very much about her so far, I have thought more of you."

"Oh, you naughty flatterer!" said the widow, graciously. "Not that I believe you. Men are such deceivers."

"Do ladies never deceive?"

"You ought to have been a lawyer, you ask such pointed questions. Really, Dr. Fenwick, I am quite afraid of you."

"There's no occasion. I am quite harmless, I do assure you. The time to be afraid of me is when you call me in as a physician."

"Excuse me, doctor, but Mrs. Gray is about to make an announcement."

We both turned our glances upon the landlady.

CHAPTER SIX
COUNT PENELLI

Mrs. Gray was a lady of the old school. She was the widow of a merchant supposed to be rich, and in the days of her magnificence had lived in a large mansion on Fourteenth Street, and kept her carriage. When her husband died suddenly of apoplexy his fortune melted away, and she found herself possessed of expensive tastes, and a pittance of *two* thousand dollars.

She was practical, however, and with a part of her money bought an old established boarding-house on Waverly Place. This she had conducted for ten years, and it yielded her a good income. Her two thousand dollars had become ten, and her future was secure.

Mrs. Gray did not class herself among boarding-house keepers. Her boarders she regarded as her family, and she felt a personal interest in each and all. When they became too deeply in arrears, they received a quiet hint, and dropped out of the pleasant home circle. But this did not happen very often.

From time to time when she had anything which she thought would interest her "family," she made what might be called a "speech from the throne." Usually we could tell when this was going to take place. She moved about a little restlessly, and pushed back her chair slightly from the table. Then all became silent and expectant.

This morning Mrs. Wyman augured rightly. Mrs. Gray was about to make an announcement.

She cleared her throat, and said: "My friends, I have a gratifying announcement to make. We are about to have an accession to our pleasant circle."

"Who is it?" asked the widow, eagerly.

Mrs. Gray turned upon her a look of silent reproof.

"It is a gentleman of high family, Count Antonio Penelli, of Italy."

There was a buzz of excitement. We had never before had a titled fellow boarder, and democratic as we were we were pleased to learn that we should sit at the same board with a nobleman.

Probably no one was more pleasantly excited than Mrs. Wyman. Every male boarder she looked upon as her constituent, if I may use this word, and she always directed her earliest efforts to captivate any new masculine arrival.

"What does he look like, Mrs. Gray?" she asked, breathless.

"He looks like an Italian," answered the landlady, in a practical tone. "He has dark hair and a dark complexion. He has also a black moustache, but no side whiskers."

"Is he good looking?"

"You will have to decide for yourselves when you see him."

"When shall we see him?"

"He is to be here tonight at supper."

"The day will seem very long," murmured the widow.

"You seem to regard him already as your special property."

This of course came from the lips of the Disagreeable Woman.

"I presume you are as anxious to see him as I am," snapped Mrs. Wyman.

"I once knew an Italian Count," said Miss Blagden reflectively.

"Did you? How nice!"

"I do not know about that. He turned out to be a barber."

"Horrible! Then he was not a count."

"I think he was, but he was poor and chose to earn a living in the only way open to him. I respected him the more on that account."

Mrs. Wyman was evidently shocked. It seemed to dissipate the halo of romance which she had woven around the coming boarder.

"Count Penelli did not appear to be in any business?" she asked, anxiously, of the landlady.

"He said he was a tourist, and wished to spend a few months in America."

The widow brightened up. This seemed to indicate that he was a man of means.

Prof. Poppendorf did not seem to share in the interest felt in the Count.

"I do not like Italians," he said. "They are light, frivolous; they are not solid like the Germans."

"The Professor is solid enough," said Mrs. Wyman, with a titter.

This could not be gainsaid, for the learned German certainly tipped the scales at over two hundred pounds. There was a strong suspicion that he imbibed copious potations of the liquid so dear to his countrymen, though he never drank it at table.

"The poor man is jealous," continued Mrs. Wyman, making the remark in a low tone for my private hearing. "He thinks we won't notice him after the Count comes."

This might be true, for Prof. Poppendorf was our star boarder. He was not supposed to be rich, but his title of Professor and his ancient intimacy with Bismarck, gave him a prestige among us all. When he first came Mrs. Wyman tried her blandishments upon him, but with indifferent success. Not that the grizzled veteran was too old for the tender passion, as we were soon to learn, but because he did not appreciate the coquettish ways of the widow, whom he considered of too light calibre for his taste.

"Don't you think the Professor very homely?" asked Mrs. Wyman, in a confidential whisper.

"He certainly is not handsome," I answered. "Neither is Bismarck."

"True, but he is a great man."

"We should respect him on account of his learning—probably much more so than the Count whom we are expecting."

"That may be. We don't expect noblemen to be learned," said the widow, disdainfully.

Immediately after breakfast she began to sound Mrs. Gray about the Count.

"When did he apply for board?" she asked.

"Yesterday afternoon about four o'clock."

"Had he heard of you? What led him here?"

"I think he saw the sign I had out."

"I should have supposed he would prefer a hotel."

"He's staying at a hotel now."

"Did he say at what hotel? Was it the Fifth Avenue?"

"He did not say. He will move here early this afternoon."

"And what room will he have?"

"The back room on the third floor—the one Mr. Bates had."

"I should hardly think that room would satisfy a nobleman."

"Why not? Is it not clean and neat?"

"Undoubtedly, dear Mrs. Gray, but you must admit that it is not stylish, and it is small."

"It is of the same size as the Professor's."

"Ah, the Professor! He is not a man of elegant tastes. I once looked into his room. It smells so strong of tobacco, I could not stay in there ten minutes without feeling sick."

"I think the Count smokes."

"Perhaps he does, but he wouldn't smoke a dirty clay pipe. I can imagine him with a dainty cigarette between his closed lips. But, Mrs. Gray, I am going to ask you a great favor."

"What is it?"

"Let me sit beside the Count. I wish to make his acquaintance. He will be reserved and silent with most of the boarders. I will try to make him feel at home."

"I thought you wished to sit beside Dr. Fenwick."

"So I did, but he and I are friends, and he won't mind my changing my seat."

When I came to supper that evening I was not wholly surprised to find myself removed to the opposite side of the table, but this I did not regret when I found that I was now next neighbor to the Disagreeable Woman.

In my old seat there was a slender young man of middle height, with dark eyes and hair. Mrs. Wyman had already established herself in confidential relations with him, and was conversing with him in a low tone.

"I suppose that is the Count," I remarked.

"At any rate he calls himself so. He has deprived you of your seat."

"Not only that but Mrs. Wyman has transferred her attentions to him."

"Doubtless to your regret?"

"Well, I don't know."

"She is scarcely off with the old love before she is on with the new," quoted Miss Blagden, with an approach to a smile.

"Perhaps you will console me," I ventured to suggest.

"I can't compete with Mrs. Wyman in her special line."

"I quite believe that," I said, smiling.

After supper the widow fluttered up to me.

"The Count is charming," she said, with enthusiasm. "He has a large estate in the South of Italy. He has come here to see the country and get acquainted with the people, and he may write a book."

"He doesn't seem overstocked with brains," observed the Disagreeable Woman. But Mrs. Wyman had fluttered away and did not hear her.

CHAPTER SEVEN
MACY'S

One day I dropped in at Macy's. I wished to make some trifling purchase. Possibly I could have bought to equal advantage elsewhere, but I was curious to see this great emporium. Years before, I had heard of it in my country home, and even then I knew just where it was located, at the corner of Fourteenth Street and Sixth Avenue.

Curious as I had been about the place, I actually spent three months in New York and had not visited it. It was something of a shock to me when I first learned there was no Macy, that the original proprietor had vanished from the stage and left his famous shop in charge of men of alien race and name. Macy had become *nominis umbra*—the shadow of a name. Yet the name had been wisely retained. Under no other name could the great store have retained its ancient and well-earned popularity.

I made my purchase—it was trifling and did not materially swell the day's receipts—and began to walk slowly about the store, taking a leisurely survey of the infinite variety of goods which it offered to the prospective purchaser.

As I was making my leisurely round, all at once I heard my name called in a low but distinct tone.

"Dr. Fenwick!"

I turned quickly, and behind the handkerchief counter I saw the young woman from Macy's, whose pleasant face I had seen so often at our table.

She nodded and smiled, and I instantly went up to the counter.

I was sensible that I must not take up the time of one of the salesladies—I believe that the genteel designation of this class—without some pretense of business, so, after greeting Ruth Canby, I said:

"You may show me some of your handkerchiefs, please."

"Do you wish something nice?" she asked.

"I wish something cheap," I answered. "It doesn't matter much what a forlorn bachelor uses."

"You may not always be a bachelor," said Ruth, with a suggestive smile.

"I must get better established in my profession before I assume new responsibilities."

"These handkerchiefs are ten cents, Dr. Fenwick," said Ruth, showing a fair article.

"I think I can go a little higher."

"And these are fifteen. They are nearly all linen."

"I will buy a couple to try," I said, by way of excusing my small purchase.

The young lady called "Cash," and soon a small girl was carrying the handkerchiefs and a fifty cent piece to the cashier. This left me five minutes for conversation, as no other customer was at hand.

"So you are in the handkerchief department?" I remarked, by way of starting a conversation.

"Yes."

"Do you like it?"

"I should prefer the book department. That is up-stairs, on the second floor. My tastes are *litery.*"

I am sure this was the word Ruth used. I was not disposed to criticize, however, only I wondered mildly how it happened that a young woman of literary tastes should make such a mistake.

"I suppose you are fond of reading?"

"Oh, yes, I have read considerable."

"What, for instance?"

"I have read one of Cooper's novels, I disremember the name, and *The Gunmaker of Moscow,* by Sylvanus Cobb, and Poe's *Tales,* but I didn't like them much, they are so queer, and—and ever so many others."

"I see you are quite a reader."

"I should read more and find out more about books if I was in the book department. A friend of mine—Mary Ann Toner—is up there, and she knows a lot about books and authors."

"Do any authors ever come in here, or rather to the book department?"

"Yes; Mary Ann told me that there was a lady with long ringlets who wrote for the story papers who came in often. She had had two books published, and always inquired how they sold."

"Do you remember her name?"

"No, I disremember."

I should like to have given her a hint that this word is hardly accounted correct, but I suspected that if I undertook to correct Miss Canby's English I should have my hands full."

"Do you think you stand a chance to get into the book department?"

"Mary Ann has agreed to speak for me when there is a vacancy. Do you often come into Macy's, Dr. Fenwick?"

"This is my first visit."

"You don't mean it? I thought everybody came to Macy's at least once a month."

"Truly it looks like it," said I, looking about and noting the crowds of customers.

"I hope you'll come again soon," said Ruth, as she turned to wait upon a lady.

"I certainly will, Miss Canby. And it won't be altogether to buy goods."

Ruth looked gratified and smiled her appreciation of the compliment. Certainly she looked comely and attractive with her rather high-colored country face, and I should have been excusable, being a bachelor, in letting my eyes rest complacently upon her rustic charms. But I was heart-proof so far as Ruth was concerned, I could not think of seeking a *litery* wife. No, she was meant for some honest but uncultured young man, whose tastes and education were commensurate with hers. And yet, as I afterwards found, Ruth had made an impresssion in a quarter quite unexpected.

I was not in search of a wife. It would have been the height of imprudence for me, with my small income and precarious prospects, to think of setting up a home and a family in this great, expensive city. Yet, had it been otherwise, perhaps Ruth would have made me a better wife than some graduate of a fashionable young ladies' seminary with her smattering of French, and superficial knowledge of the various ologies taught in high-class schools. The young woman from Macy's, though she probably knew nothing of political economy, was doubtless skilled in household economy and able to cook a dinner, as in all probability my wife would find it necessary to do.

As we entered the room at supper, Miss Canby smiled upon me pleasantly.

"I hope you are pleased with your handkerchiefs, Dr. Fenwick."

"I have not had occasion to use them as yet, thank you."

"Aha, what is that?" asked Prof. Poppendorf, who was just behind us.

"Dr. Fenwick called to see me at Macy's," answered Ruth.

Prof. Poppendorf frowned a little, as if not approving the visit.

"Do you have gentlemen call upon you at Macy's, Mees Ruth?" he asked.

"Only when they wish to buy articles," said Ruth, smiling and blushing.

"What do you sell, Mees Ruth?"

"Handkerchiefs, Professor."

"Do you have any like this?" and he pulled out a large red silk handkerchief.

"No, I have only white linen handkerchiefs."

"I haf never use any but red ones, but I might come in and see what you have."

"I shall be glad to show you what I have, Professor."

Prof. Poppendorf was soon engaged in the discussion of dinner. He had a good German appetite which never failed. He seldom talked much during a meal, as it would interfere with more important business.

Now that I had changed my place at the table, I sat one side of the Disagreeable Woman, and Ruth Canby on the other. Next to Ruth sat the Professor, but for the reason already stated, he was not a social companion.

Just opposite sat Mrs. Wyman and Count Penelli. So far as I could judge, he was a quiet young man, and had very little to say for himself. Mrs. Wyman, however, kept plying him with questions and remarks, and did her best to appear on terms of intimate acquaintance with him. Some fragments of her conversation floated across the table.

"You have no idea, Count, how I long to visit Italy, your dear country."

"It is ver' nice," he said, vaguely.

"Nice? It must be lovely. Have you ever seen the Bay of Naples?"

"Oh, *si*, signora, many times."

"It is charming, is it not?"

"*Si*, signora, it is beautiful."

"And the Italian ladies, I have heard so much of them."

"I like ze American ladies better."

"Do you, indeed, Count? How gratifying! When do you expect to return to Italy?"

"I do not know—some time."

"I hope it will not be for a long time. We should miss you so much."

"The signora is very kind."

This will do for a sample of the conversation between the Count and the widow. Though several years his senior, it looked as if she was bent on making a conquest of the young nobleman.

CHAPTER EIGHT
THE PROFESSOR IN LOVE

I was sitting in my office one morning waiting for patients, much of my time was passed in this way, very often I waited in vain. The modest sign which I was allowed to put on the outside of the house,

Dr. James Fenwick

didn't seem to attract attention. Of the little practice I had, at least a third was gratuitous. Yet I was expected to pay my bills, and when my little stock of money was exhausted there seemed a doubt as to whether the bills would be paid at all.

One day I was summoned to a house where a child of three was struggling with croup. It was a serious case, and I gave up my time to the case. After several hours I succeeded in bringing the child round and pronouncing her out of danger.

When I sent in my bill, the mother said:

"Dr. Fenwick, Mary is but three years old."

"Indeed!" I returned.

I failed to understand why I should be informed of this fact.

"And," continued the mother, "I don't think any charge ought to be made for a child so young."

I was fairly struck dumb with amazement at first.

Then I said, "The age of the patient has nothing to do with a physician's charges. Where did you get such an extraordinary idea?"

"I don't have to pay for her on the horse-cars."

"Madam," I said, provoked, "I will not argue with you. You ought to know that no physician treats children free. If you were very poor, and lived in a tenement house, I might make some discount, or leave off the charge altogether."

"But I don't live in a tenement house," objected the lady, angrily.

"No; you have the appearance of being very well-to-do. I must distinctly decline abating my charge."

"Then, Dr. Fenwick," said the mother, stiffly, "I shall not employ you again."

"That is as you please, madam."

This seemed to me exceptionally mean, but doctors see a good deal of the mean side of human nature. Rich men with large incomes keep them out of their pay for a long time, sometimes where their lives depended on the physician's skill and fidelity. Oftentimes I have been so disgusted with the meanness of my patients, that I have regretted not choosing a different profession. Of course there is a different side to the picture, and gratitude and appreciation are to be found, as well as the opposite qualities.

I had been waiting a long time without a patient, when a shuffling sound was heard on the stairs, and a heavy step approaching the door.

Next came a knock.

Instead of calling out, "Come in!" I was so pleased at the prospect of a patient, that I rose from my seat and opened the door, myself.

I started back in surprise. For in the heavy, lumbering figure of the new arrival I recognized Prof. Poppendorf.

"Prof. Poppendorf!" I exclaimed.

"*Ja,* doctor, it is I. May I come in?"

"Certainly."

Supposing that he had come to consult me on the subject of his health, I began to wonder from what disease he was suffering. Remembering his achievements at the table I fancied it might be dyspepsia.

The Professor entered the room, and sank into an armchair, which he quite filled from side to side.

"I suppose you are surprised to see me, Herr Doctor," began the Professor.

"Oh, no. I am never surprised to see anybody. I had not supposed you were sick."

"Sick! Oh, no, I'm all right. I eat well and I sleep well. What should be the matter with me?"

"I am glad to hear such good reports of you."

Was I quite sincere? I am afraid it was a disappointment to learn that my supposed patient was in no need of advice.

"*Ja,* I am well. I was never better, thank God!"

"Then I am to consider this a social call," I said with affected cheerfulness. "You are very kind to call upon me, Prof. Poppendorf. I appreciate it as a friendly attention."

"No, it is not quite dat."

"Is there anything I can do for you?"

"I come on a little peezness."

I was puzzled. I could not understand what business there could be between the Professor and myself.

"I shall be glad to hear what it is."

"You see, I thought I would ask you if you were courting Mees Ruth Canby, if you mean to make her your wife?"

I dropped into the nearest chair—I had been standing—in sheer amazement. To be asked my intentions in regard to the young woman from Macy's was most astonishing, and by Prof. Poppendorf, too!

"Did Miss Canby send you here to speak to me?" I asked, considerably annoyed.

"Oh, no! She knows nothing about it."

"I can't understand what you have to do in the matter, Prof. Poppendorf. You are neither her father nor her brother."

"Oh, *ja,* you are quite right."

"Then why do you come to me with such a question?"

"I thought I would like to know myself."

"I deny your right to speak to me on the subject," I said, stiffly. "If now you had a good reason."

"But I have a reason," protested the Professor, earnestly.

"What is it?"

"I lofe her myself. I wish to make her my frau."

This was most astonishing.

"You love her yourself?"

"*Ja,* Herr Doctor."

"And you want to marry her?"

"*Ja.*"

"But you are an old man."

"Not so old," said he, jealously; "I am only a little over sixty."

"And I think she cannot be over twenty-one."

"But I am a good man. I am strong. I am well. Look here!" And he struck his massive chest a sturdy blow, as if to show how sound he was.

"Yes, you seem to be well."

"You have not told me, Herr Doctor, if you lofe Mees Ruth," he said, uneasily.

"No, I don't love her."

"But you called to see her—at Macy's."

"I called to buy some socks and handkerchiefs."

"Was that all?" he asked, with an air of relief.

"It was all."

"Then you do not wish to marry Mees Ruth?"

"I do not wish to marry any one. I am not rich enough. Are you?"

"I have just engage to teach philosophy at Mees Smith's school on Madison Avenue. Then I have my private pupils. Ah, *ja,* I will make quite an income," he said, complacently. "Besides, Mees Ruth, she is a good housekeeper."

"I do not know."

"She will not wish to spend money," he said, anxiously.

"I think she was brought up economically."

"*Ja,* dat is good. All the German frauleins are good housekeepers. Dey can cook and keep house on a little money."

"Were you ever married, Professor?"

"*Ja,* long ago, but my frau she not live very long. It is many years ago."

"If you married Miss Canby would you still board here?"

"No, it would cost too much money. I would hire an apartment—what you call a flat, and Mees Ruth would keep the house—she would wash, she would cook, and——"

"Take care of the babies," I added, jocularly.

"Dat is as God wills."

"Have you spoken to Miss Ruth on the subject?"

"No, not yet. I wish to speak to you first—I thought you might want to marry her yourself."

"You need have no anxiety on that subject; I never thought of such a thing."

"Dat is good. I feel better."

"Have you any idea that Miss Canby will agree to marry you?"

"I do not know. I am a Herr Professor," he said, proudly.

In Germany there is a high respect felt for titles of every kind, and the Professor evidently thought that his official dignity would impress the young woman from Macy's.

"Still, you are so much older than she, that she may not at first like the idea."

"You think she refuse me—that she gives me the mitten?" he said, uneasily.

"If you propose too quick. Will you take my advice?"

"*Ja, ja!*"

"Then don't propose at once. Let her get accustomed to your attentions."

"What shall I do first?" he asked, anxiously.

"Suppose you invite her to go to the theatre with you?"

"*Ja,* dat is good!"

"Perhaps you could take her to hear Patti?"

"No, no. It cost too much!" said he, shaking his head.

"Then you might invite her to the Star Theatre to see Crane."

"So I will."

He rose and shuffled out of the office in a very pleasant humor.

He felt that there was no obstacle to his suit, now that I had disclaimed all intention of marrying the young woman from Macy's.

CHAPTER NINE
AN EVENING AT THE BOARDING-HOUSE

The confidence which Prof. Poppendorf had reposed in me, naturally led me to observe his behavior at table to the young woman from Macy's. There was a difficulty as I had to look round the "Disagreeable Woman," who sat next to me. Then I could not very well watch the Professor's expression, as his large, green goggles concealed so large a part of his face.

He still continued to devote the chief part of his time to the business of the hour, and his eyes were for the most part fixed upon his plate. Yet now and then I observed he offered her the salt or the pepper, a piece of attention quite new to him. I had some thought of suggesting to Miss Canby that she had awakened an interest in the heart of the gray old Professor, but it occurred to me that this would be hardly fair to the elderly suitor. It was only right to leave him a fair field, and let him win if Fate ordained it.

On Wednesday evenings it was generally understood that the boarders, such at any rate as had no other engagements, would remain after supper and gather in the little reception-room, till the dining-room was cleared, spending the evening socially.

On such occasions Mrs. Wyman would generally volunteer a song, accompanying herself if there was no one else to play. She had a thin, strident voice, such as one would not willingly hear a second time, but out of courtesy we listened, and applauded. The widow had one who fully appreciated her vocal efforts, and this was herself. She always looked pleased and complacent when her work was done.

It was on the first Wednesday after the Count's arrival that she induced him to remain.

"Don't you sing, Count?" she asked.

"Very little, madam," he said.

"But you are an Italian, and all Italians are musical."

He uttered a faint disclaimer, but she insisted.

"Do me a favor—a great favor," she said, persuasively, "and sing some sweet Italian air, such as you must know."

"No, I don't sing Italian airs," he said.

"What then?"

"I can sing 'Sweet Marie.'"

"I am sure we shall all be glad to hear it. I sometimes sing a little myself—just a tiny bit."

"I shall like much to hear you, signora."

"I shall feel very bashful about singing to an Italian gentleman. You will laugh at me."

"No, no, I would not be so rude."

"Then perhaps I may. Our friends always insist upon hearing me."

So at an early period in the evening she sang one of her routine songs.

I watched the Count's face while she was singing. I was amused. At first his expression was one of surprise. Then of pain, and it seemed to me of annoyance. When Mrs. Wyman had completed the song she turned to him a look of complacent inquiry. She was looking for a complement.

"Didn't I do horribly?" she asked.

"Oh, no, no," answered the Count, vaguely.

"It must have seemed very bad to you."

"No, no——"

"Do you think it was passable?"

"Oh, signora, I never heard anything like it."

"Oh, you naughty flatterer," she said, smiling with delight. "I am sure you don't mean it."

"Indeed I do."

I was sitting next the Disagreeable Woman.

"The Count has more brains than I thought," she said. "I quite agree with him."

"That you never heard anything like it?" I queried, smiling.

"Yes."

"Miss Ruth," I said to the young woman from Macy's, "do you never sing?"

"I used to sing a little in my country home," she admitted.

"What, for instance?"

"I can sing Annie Laurie."

"Nothing could be better. It is a general favorite. Won't you sing it tonight?"

"But I cannot sing without an accompaniment," she said, shyly.

"I am not much of a musician, but I can play that."

With a little more persuasion I induced her to sing. She had a pleasant voice, and while I cannot claim for her anything out of the common on the score of musical talent, she rendered the song fairly well. All seemed to enjoy it, except Mrs. Wyman, who said, in a sneering tone:

"That song is old as the hills."

"It may be so," I retorted, "but the best songs are old."

"It was very good," said the Count, who really seemed pleased.

This seemed to annoy the widow.

"You are very good-natured, Count, to compliment such a rustic performance," she said.

"But, signora, I mean it."

"Well, let it pass! She did her best, poor thing!"

"She is a nice girl."

"Oh, Count, she is only a young woman from Macy's. She was born in the country, and raised among cabbages and turnips."

He seemed puzzled, but evidently regarded Ruth with favor.

Meanwhile, Prof. Poppendorf had listened attentively to the song of the maiden on whom he had fixed his choice.

"Mees Ruth, you sing beautiful!" he said.

Ruth Canby smiled.

"You are very kind, Prof. Poppendorf," she said, gratefully.

"I like your singing much better than Mrs. Wyman's."

"No. You mustn't say that. She sings airs from the opera."

"I like better your leetle song."

By this time Mrs. Wyman had succeeded in extracting a promise from the Count to sing.

"Dr. Fenwick," she said, "can't you play the accompaniment for the Count?"

"What is the song?"

" 'Sweet Marie.' "

"I will do my best. I am not professional."

So I played and the Count sang. He had a pleasant, sympathetic voice, and we were pleased with his singing.

"Oh, how charming, Count!" said Mrs. Wyman; "I shall never dare to sing before you again."

"Why not, signora."

"Because you are such a musical artist."

"Oh, no, no, signora!" he said, deprecatingly.

He was persuaded to sing again, and again he pleased his small audience.

"Miss Blagden, won't you favor us with a song?" asked Mrs. Wyman, in a tone of mockery.

"Thank you," said the Disagreeable Woman, dryly. "There is so much musical talent here, that I won't undertake to compete with those who possess it."

"Prof. Poppendorf, don't you ever sing?" asked the widow, audaciously.

"I used to sing when I was young," answered the Professor, unexpectedly.

"Then *do* favor us!"

He seated himself at the piano, and sang a German drinking song, such as in days gone by he had sung with Bismarck and his old comrades at the university.

There was a rough vigor in his performance that was not unpleasant. No one was more surprised than Mrs. Wyman at the outcome of what she had meant as a joke.

"Really, Professor," said the Disagreeable Woman, "you are more accomplished than I supposed. I like your song better than I did your lecture."

Prof. Poppendorf removed his glasses, and we saw in his eyes a suspicious moisture.

"Ah," he said, not appearing to hear the compliment, if it was a compliment, "it brings back the old days. I have not sing that song since I was at the university with Bismarck. There were twenty of us, young students, who sang it together, and now they are almost all gone."

This ended the musical performances of the evening. After this, there was conversation, and later Mrs. Gray provided ice-cream and cake. It was Horton's ice-cream, and the plates were small, but we enjoyed it.

Before we parted, the Professor found himself sitting next to Ruth Canby.

"Do you ever go to the theatre, fraulein?" he asked.

"Not often, Professor. I cannot go alone, and there is no one to take me."

"I will take you, Mees Ruth."

The young woman from Macy's looked amazed. She had not dreamed of such an invitation from him. Yet she was very fond of the stage, and she saw no reason why she should not accept.

"You are very kind, Professor," she said. "I did not think you cared for the theatre."

"I would like to go—with you," he said, gallantly.

"Then I will go."

It will be like going with my grandfather, she thought.

CHAPTER TEN
A RUSTIC ADMIRER

Sunday was always a lonely day to me. In the country village, where I knew everybody, I always looked forward to it as the pleasantest day of the week. Here in the crowded city, I felt isolated from human sympathy. I accustomed myself to attending church in the forenoon. In the afternoon I took a walk or an excursion.

At the boarding-house even it was dull and less social than usual. Such of the boarders as had friends near the city were able to absent themselves after breakfast. Among the faces that I missed was that of the Disagreeable Woman. Sometimes she appeared at breakfast; but never at dinner or tea. Though she never indulged in conversation to any extent, I think we all missed her.

One Sunday afternoon, soon after the gathering described in the last chapter, I walked up Fifth Avenue to Central Park. It was a pleasant day and many were out. Through the magnificent avenue I walked in a leisurely way, and wondered idly how it would seem to own a residence in this aristocratic street. I could not repress a feeling of envy when I thought of the favored class who dwelt in the long line of palaces that line the avenue. Their lives seemed far removed from that of a struggling physician, who was in daily doubt how long he could maintain his modest style of living in the crowded metropolis.

Arriving at Fifty-ninth Street I sauntered toward the menagerie. This is the favorite resort of children, and of young persons from the country. Perhaps I, myself, might be classed among the latter. I did not care so much, however, to observe the animals as the visitors. I had a hope that I might see some one whom I knew.

At first I could see no familiar face. But presently I started, as my glance fell on the short and somewhat plump figure of the young woman from Macy's.

She was not alone. With her walked a tall, sun-burned young man, who was evidently from the country. She leaned confidingly upon his arm, and her face was radiant. He was evidently an old friend, perhaps a lover. He, too, looked contented and happy. Were they lovers? It looked like it. If so, the matrimonial plans of Prof. Poppendorf were doomed to disappointment. Delicacy dictated my silent withdrawal, but I confess that my curiosity was aroused, and I resolved to gratify it.

Accordingly I pressed forward and overtook the young woman from Macy's and her escort. She looked up casually, and a little flush overspread her face when she recognized me.

"Dr. Fenwick!" she said, impulsively.

I turned and lifted my hat.

"I am glad to meet you, Miss Canby!" I said.

At the same time I looked inquiringly at her escort.

"Stephen," she said, "this is Dr. Fenwick from our boarding-house."

"Proud to know you, sir," said the young man, offering his hand.

I shook it heartily.

"You have not mentioned your friend's name, Miss Canby," I said.

"Excuse me! I am very neglectful. This is Stephen Higgins from our town. I used to go to school with him."

"I am glad to make your acquaintance, Mr. Higgins."

"Same to you, sir."

"I suppose you are on a visit to the city, Mr. Higgins."

"Yes, sir. I came here to spend Sunday, and see Ruth."

"I presume you have been in the city before?"

"Not for five years. It's a pretty smart place. I'm so turned round that I hardly know which way to turn."

"You will have a good guide in Miss Canby."

"In Ruth, yes."

"I wish I could go round with him all the time he is here, Dr. Fenwick, but tomorrow I shall have to go back to my work at Macy's."

She gave a little sigh as she spoke.

"Do you intend to stay long, Mr. Higgins?"

"Only a day or two. It's pretty expensive stayin' in York."

"I want him to stay over till Tuesday, Dr. Fenwick. He can't see much if he goes home tomorrow."

"If you could be with me, Ruth——"

"But I can't, so it's no use talking about it."

"Wouldn't Mr. Macy give you a day off?"

"If I could find him perhaps he would," she said, laughing.

"Why can't you find him? Isn't he at the store every day?"

"Mr. Macy is dead, Stephen."

"Then how can he keep store?" asked Stephen, bewildered.

"Somebody else runs it in his name?"

"Don't let me interfere with your plans," I said, feeling that perhaps I might be in the way.

They both urged me to stay, and so I did.

By this time all the attractions of the menagerie had been seen, and I proposed to walk to the lake.

"How would you like to live in the city, Mr. Higgins?" I asked.

"First rate, if I could find anything to do."

"What is your business at home?"

"I work on father's farm. Next year, as father's gettin' feeble, I may take it on shares."

"That will be better, perhaps, than seeking a situation in the city."

"I should like to be here on account of Ruth," he said wistfully.

She smiled and shook her head.

"There's nothing for me to do in the country," she said.

"I might find something for you to do," he said, eagerly.

Then I saw how it was, and felt inclined to help him.

"Do you like Macy's so well, then?" I asked.

"I don't know," she answered, thoughtfully, "I like to feel that I am earning my living."

"You wouldn't need," commenced Stephen, but she checked him by a look.

"You might not like to part with the Professor," said I, mischievously.

Stephen took instant alarm.

"What Professor?" he asked.

"Professor Poppendorf. He is a German, a very learned man."

"And what have you got to do with the Professor, Ruth?" he asked, jealously.

"Oh, you foolish boy!" she said. "You ought to see him."

"I don't want to see him."

"He is an old gentleman, most seventy, and wears green glasses."

Stephen looked relieved.

"By the way, did you have a pleasant evening with the Professor at the theatre the other evening, Miss Canby?"

It was very reprehensible of me, I know, but I felt a little mischievous.

"Did you go to the theatre with him, Ruth?" asked Stephen, reproachfully.

"Yes, I am so fond of the theatre, you know, I could not resist the temptation."

"What did you see?"

"I went to see Crane in *The Senator.* Where do you think we sat?" and she laughed.

"I don't know."

"In the upper gallery. The idea of asking a lady to sit in the top of the house!"

"The Professor is a German, and all Germans are frugal. I presume he thought you would be perfectly satisfied. Did the Professor appear to enjoy the play?"

"Very much. He did not always understand it, and asked me to explain it to him. Now and then he burst into such a loud laugh that I felt quite ashamed. Then I was glad that we were in the top gallery."

"When the play was over did he invite you to take an ice-cream at Delmonico's or Maillard's?"

"No, but he invited me into a saloon to take a glass of lager."

Here she laughed again.

"Evidently the Professor is not a ladies' man. Did you accept the beer?"

"As if I would!"

"Poor man! you deprived him of a pleasure."

"No, I did not. He left me on the sidewalk while he went in and took his beer."

"I hope you won't go to the theatre with him again," said Stephen, in a tone of dissatisfaction.

"You can rest quite easy, Stephen, I won't."

"What made him ask you to go?"

"You will have to ask him, Stephen. If you will come round to supper this evening, I will introduce you to him. There will be plenty of room, as some of our boarders are always away on Sunday."

Stephen felt a little bashful at first, but finally yielded to persuasion and took his place at the table in the seat of the Disagreeable Woman.

After seeing the Professor he got over his jealousy. The old German scholar hardly suggested a young Lothario, and his appearance was not calculated to excite jealousy. Prof. Poppendorf removed his goggles the better to observe Ruth's friend, but did not appear to be disturbed. That Ruth should prefer this young rustic to a man of his position and attainments, would have seemed to him quite out of the range of probability.

CHAPTER ELEVEN
A POOR PATIENT

I was accustomed to remain in my office till about four o'clock in the afternoon waiting for possible patients. It was a long and weary wait, and oftentimes not a caller rewarded me. I suppose it is the usual fortune of young medical practitioners who are comparatively unknown. When four o'clock came I went out for a walk. Generally my steps tended to Sixth Avenue where there was some life and bustle.

I was compelled to practice the most rigid economy, but I could not deny myself the luxury of an evening paper. I would buy either the *Sun* or *World,* each of which cost but a penny. One little newsboy came to know me, and generally lay in wait for me as I emerged from a side street. He was a bright, attractive little boy of ten, whose name I found to be Frank Mills. His clothing was well-worn but clean, and his whole appearance was neat, so that I judged he had a good mother.

Usually Frank's manner was cheerful, but on the day succeeding my visit to the Park I found he looked sober and his eyes looked red as if he had been crying.

"What is the matter, Frank?" I asked.

"My sister is sick," he said, sadly.

"Is it an older sister?"

"Yes; she works at O'Neil's dry goods store. She has been sick two days."

"What is the matter?"

"Mother thinks it is a fever."

"Have you called a doctor?"

"N—no," answered Frank.

"Why not?"

"We haven't any money to pay a doctor. We are very poor, and now that sister isn't working I don't know how we shall get along. There is no one to earn money except me, and I don't make more than thirty cents a day."

"If I were rich, Frank, I would help you."

"I am sure you would, sir, for you look like a kind gentleman."

This simple tribute went to my heart. The boy felt that I was a friend, and I determined that I would be one so far as I was able.

"Still I can do something for you. I am a doctor, and if you will take me round to your house I will look at your sister and see if I can do anything for her."

The boy's eyes lighted up with joy.

"Will you be so kind, sir? I will go with you now."

"Yes, Frank, the sooner the better."

I followed him for perhaps a quarter of a mile to a poor house situated on one of the side streets leading down to the North River. The street was shabby enough, and the crowd of young children playing about showed that it was tenanted by poor families, rich in children if nothing else.

Frank stopped at one of these houses and opened the door into a dirty hall.

"We live on the top floor," he said, "if you won't mind going up."

"I shall mind it no more than you, Frank," I said. "I am still a young man."

We climbed three staircases, and stood on the upper landing.

"I'll go in and tell mother I have brought a doctor," said Frank. "Just wait here a minute."

He opened a door and entered. He came out again almost immediately. He was followed by a woman of perhaps forty, with a pleasant face, but looking very sad.

"Welcome, doctor," she said. "Frank tells me you were kind enough to offer us your services."

"Yes, I am glad to do what I can for you."

"This is my daughter. I feel very much worried about her."

The daughter lay on a bed in an inner room (there were but two).

She was pale and looked ill-nourished, but in spite of the delicacy of her appearance, she was pretty.

"Alice, this is the doctor," said her mother. Alice opened her eyes languidly, and tried to smile.

"Let me feel your pulse," I said.

The pulsations were slow and feeble.

The mother fixed her eyes upon me anxiously, and awaited my verdict.

"Your daughter is quite run down," I said. "She has very little strength, but I do not find any positive indications of disease."

"You are right, no doubt, doctor," said the mother with a sigh. "She is a delicate girl, and I am sure she was overworked."

"She is employed in a dry goods store, Frank tells me."

"Yes, she is at O'Neil's. They are very considerate there, but it is hard to be standing all day."

"It would be hard for any one. I am a man and strong, but I don't think I could endure it. She ought to have two weeks' rest, at least, before returning to work."

"I am sure you are right, doctor," said Mrs. Mills, "but how can it be managed? We have but two breadwinners, Frank and Alice. Frank, poor boy, brings in all he can, but Alice earns six dollars a week. It is upon that that we depend for our living. It is a hard thing to be poor, doctor."

"Indeed it is," I answered.

"You speak as if you know something about it."

"I do. I am a young physician, with very little money, and few patients. Life with me is a struggle, as it is with you."

I was well dressed—that is a necessity with a professional man, who must keep up appearances—and this perhaps made it difficult for Mrs. Mills to believe that I was really poor.

"What do you prescribe, doctor?"

"No medicines are needed. What your daughter needs most is strengthening food—to begin with a little beef tea."

Mrs. Mills looked embarrassed. I understood her embarrassment. What I ordered was simple enough; but where was the money to come from, to supply the sick girl's needs?

"I can make some beef tea," she said, after a pause, "and some bread."

"It is just the thing," I said, cheerfully.

"Then you don't think she needs any medicine?"

"No."

There was still that anxious look on the mother's face. Alice was the breadwinner, and she was sick. How were they to live?

An idea came to me.

"I will call again tomorrow morning," I said, cheerfully.

"You are very kind, doctor. I should like to pay you, but we are so miserably poor."

"Don't let that trouble you for a moment. I can give you some of my time, for of that I have plenty."

CHAPTER TWELVE
THE DISAGREEABLE WOMAN IN A NEW LIGHT

I have said that I had an idea. The destitute condition of this poor family weighed upon me, and excited my sympathy. With my scanty means I could give them only advice, but could I not secure help from others?

Mrs. Gray, my landlady, would perhaps furnish a supply of food, but though a good woman in the main she was not inclined to be charitable. She was inclined to be suspicious of those who applied to her for help, and I did not want to subject Mrs. Mills to any new sorrow or mortification. Among my fellow boarders, I could not think of one to whom I could apply, except—well, yes, except the Disagreeable Woman. Under her cynical exterior I suspected there was a sympathetic heart, though I believe that I alone gave her credit for it. I resolved to speak to her about my poor patient.

As the reader already knows, I sat next to Miss Blagden at the table. Toward the close of supper I said in a low voice: "If you will allow me, Miss Blagden, I will walk with you a short distance after supper. I have something to say to you."

She looked surprised, but answered promptly, "I shall be glad of your company."

This was the most agreeable speech I had heard from her since our acquaintance commenced.

Nothing more was said till I found myself walking by her side toward Broadway.

"Now?" she said, expectantly.

"I am going to take a liberty," I said. "I am going to try to interest you in a poor family. I of course know nothing of your means, but my own are so limited that in spite of my profound sympathy I can only give my medical services, while more is needed."

"Go on, doctor," she said, and there was unwonted kindness in her tone.

I told her the story in brief words, and she seemed interested.

"Your young patient has no organic disease?" she inquired.

"None whatever. She is ill-nourished, and works too hard. That is the whole story."

"They are very poor."

"You can judge. Their income cannot be more than seven dollars and a half, and of this the girl earns six dollars. Her sickness will entail some outlay, and there is only the boy to earn money now."

"It is very sad, doctor. How little we whose wants are provided for know of the sufferings of the poor! But fortunately," she added, and a rare smile lighted up her features and made her positively attractive, in spite of her name, "fortunately there is a remedy. When do you see this poor family again?"

"I shall call tomorrow morning after breakfast."

"And in the meantime do you think they will suffer for the lack of food?"

"It may be so. I don't think they have much money in the house."

"Do you think you could make it convenient to call there this evening?"

"Yes, I am sure I could. Their poor home is less than half a mile distant from our boarding-house."

"Then, doctor, be kind enough to hand them this."

She drew out her purse and handed me a five dollar bill.

I suppose I showed the joy I felt.

"Miss Blagden," I said, "you could not give me a more agreeable commission."

"I believe it, doctor."

There was an unwonted softness in her tone, and her smile was positively attractive.

How could we call her the "Disagreeable Woman?"

CHAPTER THIRTEEN
MRS. WYMAN'S CURIOSITY

I was passing our boarding-house on my return from the walk with Miss Blagden when Mrs. Wyman tapped on the window, and opened it.

"I saw you!" she said, in a bantering tone.

"At supper?"

"No, I saw you walking away with Miss Blagden. So you are smitten at last!"

I smiled.

"I assure you," I said, "there is nothing between us."

"You seem uncommonly attentive," and I thought there was something of pique in her tone.

"What can I do?" I answered. "You have forsaken me, and devote yourself to the Count."

"As if I could forget you!" she said, in a sentimental tone.

If she had known how utterly indifferent I was to her favor or disfavor she would hardly have been complimented. She had transferred her attentions to Count Penelli, but she still wished to retain her hold upon me.

"By the way," she said, suddenly, "are you going to hear Patti during her present engagement?"

"Do you take me for a millionaire?"

"Her prices are frightful!" she said, thoughtfully. "Of course I cannot go without an escort."

"If you will secure two tickets, I will accompany you."

"Thank you, but I am so poor. Still I dote on music, and I would buy my own ticket."

I shrugged my shoulders, and declined to take the hint.

"Very probably the Count will wish to go. He is an Italian, you know, and would have the advantage of understanding the language."

"True."

"As a nobleman he is doubtless above money considerations."

"You are mistaken. He is the heir to great estates, but he is out of favor with his father, and has to live on a very small allowance. It is a pity, isn't it?"

"He might work at some business, and replenish his purse."

"But you must remember he is a nobleman. His rank debars him from many positions that would be open to a common man."

"I am glad that I am not a nobleman, then."

"Ah, he might not object to being a doctor if he were trained to that profession. I wish there were any way of getting a ticket to Patti, without such a monstrous outlay. Can't you think of any way?"

"Mr. Blake is connected with a morning paper. Perhaps he may be entitled to a Press ticket."

"Thank you, Dr. Fenwick. That is an excellent suggestion. I will speak to him tomorrow morning. Where are you walking, if I may ask?"

"To see a poor patient. Will you accompany me?"

"No, no, I should be afraid of catching some horrid fever or something."

"The family is poor, and stands very much in need of assistance."

"How will they pay you, then?"

"They won't pay me. I shall not ask any compensation."

"I think you are foolish to waste your time on such people. They can't benefit you."

"I can help them."

"You will never get rich in that way."

"I do not expect to. I shall be satisfied if I can make a living. If you feel inclined to be charitable, I can recommend Mrs. Mills as deserving all the help you are inclined to bestow."

"I positively haven't a cent to spare. Besides it would make it all the more difficult to hear Patti."

Mrs. Wyman closed the window. The conversation had taken a turn which she did not relish.

CHAPTER FOURTEEN
THE QUALITY OF MERCY

When I knocked again at the door of Mrs. Mills, she opened it and regarded me in some surprise.

"Did you think Alice would be worse?" she asked.

"No, but I am commissioned by a charitable lady, one of my fellow boarders, to give you this."

She took the bill which I offered her, and her face lighted up with joy.

"It is a godsend," she said. "I was feeling very anxious. We had but twenty-five cents in the house."

"This will help along."

"Indeed it will. How kind you are, doctor," and her eyes filled with grateful tears.

"I would like to be kind, but my ability is limited."

"And who is this lady to whom I am indebted?"

"We call her the Disagreeable Woman."

She looked very much surprised.

"Surely you are jesting, doctor."

"No; she is a social mystery. She is very blunt and says many sharp things."

"But she sends me this money. She must have a good heart."

"I begin to think so. It would surprise all at the table if they knew she had done this."

"I shall think of her as the Agreeable Woman."

"Now, Mrs. Mills, I am going to give you some advice. What your daughter needs is nourishing food. Use this money to provide it not only for her but for yourself."

"I will—but when this is gone," she hesitated.

"We will appeal to the Disagreeable Woman. What has your daughter taken?"

"I have given her some beef tea."

"That is good as far as it goes. Do you think she could eat a bit of steak?"

"I will ask her."

Alice seemed so pleased at the suggestion that Frank was dispatched to the butcher's for a pound of sirloin steak, and a few potatoes. Soon the rich and appetizing flavor of broiled steak pervaded the apartment, and a smile of contentment lighted up the face of the sick girl.

"Now mind that you and Frank eat some too," I said. "I will see you tomorrow morning.

I made a report to Miss Blagden at breakfast.

"If you had seen how much pleasure your gift gave, you would feel amply repaid," I said to her.

"Doctor," she said, earnestly, "I thank you for mentioning this case to me. We are so apt to live for ourselves."

"I also mentioned the case to Mrs. Wyman," I added.

"Well?" she asked, curiously.

"She said she was very poor, and wanted to buy a ticket to Patti's concert."

Miss Blagden smiled.

"I am not surprised to hear it," she said. "Did you ever hear Patti, Dr. Fenwick?"

"No, Miss Blagden. I am new to the city, and I am cut off from expensive amusements by my limited means."

"Do you like music?"

"Very much. When Patti gives a concert at fifty cents, I may venture to go."

At supper Miss Blagden placed something in my hand.

I looked at it, and found that it was a ticket to Patti's concert on the following evening. It would give me admission to the most expensive part of the house.

"You are very kind, Miss Blagden," I said, in grateful surprise.

"Don't mention where you got it. You may consider it in the light of a fee for attendance upon your poor patient. By the way, how is she? Have you been there today?"

"Yes; she is doing well, but is in a great hurry to get well. The rent comes due next week, and——"

"How much is it?" asked Miss Blagden interrupting me.

"Seven dollars."

She drew a ten dollar bill from her pocket-book and extended it to me.

"Give that to Mrs. Mills," she said.

"You make me very happy as well as her; I am beginning to find how kind and charitable you are."

"No, no," she said gravely. "There are few of us of whom that may be said. How soon do you think your patient will be able to resume work?"

"Next Monday, I hope. She is gaining rapidly."

"How thick you are with the Disagreeable Woman!" said Mrs. Wyman, when she next met me. "Don't fail to invite me to the wedding."

"On one condition."

"What is that?"

"That you invite me to your wedding with the Count."

She smiled complacently and called me a naughty man. I wonder if she aspires to become a Countess.

CHAPTER FIFTEEN
THE PROFESSOR'S COURTSHIP

"What a guy!"

The busy day at Macy's was over. Troops of young women passed through the doors, in street costume, and laughing and chatting, made their way up or down Sixth Avenue, or turned into Twenty-third Street. Among them was Ruth Canby, and it was to her that her friend Maria Stevenson addressed the above exclamation.

Ruth turned to observe the figure indicated by her friend, and was almost speechless with surprise.

At the corner leaning against the lamppost was a figure she knew well. The rusty overcoat with its amplitude of cape, the brown crushed hat, the weather-beaten face, and the green goggles were unmistakable. It was Prof. Poppendorf. He was peering in his short-sighted way at the young women emerging from the great store with an inquiring gaze. Suddenly his eyes brightened. He had found the object of his search.

"Mees Ruth!" he exclaimed, stepping forward briskly, "I haf come to walk home with you."

Ruth looked confused and almost distressed. She would gladly have found some excuse to avoid the walk but could think of none.

"Maria!" she said, hurriedly, "it is an old friend of the family. I shall have to leave you."

Her friend looked at the rusty figure in amazement.

"Oh, well, Ruth," she said, "we will meet tomorrow. So long!"

This was not perhaps the way in which a Fifth Avenue maiden would have parted from her friend, but Maria Stevenson was a free and easy young woman, of excellent heart and various good qualities, but lacking the social veneering to be met with in a different class of society.

"How provoking!" thought Ruth, as she reluctantly took her place beside the Professor, who, unlike herself, seemed in the best of spirits.

"I haf waited here a quarter of an hour to meet you, Mees Ruth," he said.

I wish you hadn't, thought Ruth, but she only said, "I am sorry to have put you to so much trouble."

"It was no trouble, I assure you, Mees Ruth," said her elderly companion in as genial a tone as his bass voice could assume.

"Let us cross the street," suggested Ruth.

She wished as soon as possible to get out of sight of her shop companions, who were sure to tease her the next day.

"With all my heart," said the Professor. "I should wish to be more alone."

They crossed Sixth Avenue, and walked down on the west side. Ruth was wondering all the while what on earth could have induced the Professor to take such pains to offer her his escort. She did not have long to wait.

"I haf something very particular to say to you, Mees Ruth," said the Professor, gazing fondly at her through his green goggles.

"Indeed!" returned Ruth, in great surprise.

"Yes, Mees Ruth, I haf been feeling very lonely. I am tired of living at a boarding-house. I wish to have a home of my own. Will you marry me? Will you be my frau—I mean my wife?"

Ruth Canby stopped short. She was "like to drop," as she afterwards expressed it.

"Marry you!" she repeated, in a dazed way.

"Yes, Mees Ruth, dear Mees Ruth, I want you to be my wife."

"But, Professor, I could never think of marrying a man so——" old she was about to add, but she feared it would hurt the Professor's feelings.

"I know what you would say, Mees Ruth. You think I am too old. But I am strong. See here!" and he smote his large breast vigorously. "I am sound, and I shall live many years. My father lived till eighty-five, and I am only sixty-five."

"I am only twenty."

"True! you are much younger, but no young man would love you so fondly."

"I don't know," said Ruth.

"Perhaps you think I am poor, but it is not so. I haf a good income, and I haf just been appointed to gif lectures on philosophy in Miss Green's school on Madison Avenue. We will take a nice flat. I will furnish it well, and we will haf a happy home."

"Thank you very much, Prof. Poppendorf," said Ruth, hurriedly. "Indeed I feel complimented that such a learned man and great scholar should wish to marry me, but I am only a simple girl—I have not much education—and I should not make a suitable wife for you."

"Do not think of that, Mees Ruth. I will teach you myself. I will teach you Latin and Greek, and Sanscrit, if you please. I will read my lectures on philosophy to you, and I will make you *'une femme savante,'* so that you can talk with my brother Professors who will come to see me. You can cook, can you not, Mees Ruth?"

"Yes, I know how to cook, but——"

"Ah, that is well," said the Professor, in a tone of satisfaction. "All the German ladies can cook. Frau von Bismarck, the wife of my old friend, is an excellent cook. I haf dined at Bismarck's house."

"But," said Ruth, firmly, "I cannot think of becoming your wife, Prof. Poppendorf."

"Ach, so!" said the Professor, in a tone of disappointment. "Do not make such a mistake, my dear Mees Ruth. Is it nothing to become Mrs. Professor Poppendorf. You will take a good place in society. For I assure you that I am well known among scholars. I am now busy on a great work on philosophy, which will extend my fame. I will make you proud of your husband."

"Indeed, Prof. Poppendorf, I do not doubt your learning or your fame, but I cannot marry a man old enough to be my grandfather."

"So, I am not so sure about that. I am old enough to be your father, but——"

"Never mind! We will not argue the point. I hope you will say no more. I cannot marry you."

"Ah! is there another? Haf I a rival?" demanded the Professor, frowning fiercely. "It is that Dr. Fenwick?"

"No, it is not."

"I do not think he would care to marry you."

"And I don't want to marry him, though I think him a very nice young gentleman."

"Who is it, then?"

"If you must know," said Ruth, pettishly, "it is that young man who took supper with us not long ago."

"The young man from the country?"

"Yes."

"But what do you see in him, Mees Ruth. He is a *yokel.*"

"A what?"

"He is a very worthy young man, I do not doubt, but what does he know? He is a farmer, is he not, with no ideas beyond his paternal acres?"

"Prof. Poppendorf, I will not have you speak so of my Stephen," said Ruth, while a wave of anger passed over her face.

"Ah, that is his name. Stephen. Pardon, Mees Ruth! I do not wish to say anything against this rural young man, but he will never give you the position which I offer you."

"Perhaps not, but I like him better."

"Ach, so. Then is my dream at an end; I did hope to have you for my frau, and haf a happy home and a loving companion in my declining years."

His tone seemed so mournful that Ruth was touched with pity and remorse.

"Prof. Poppendorf," she said, gently, "you must not be too much disappointed. There are many who would appreciate the honor of marrying you. Why do you not ask Mrs. Wyman?"

"She is a butterfly—a flirt. I would not marry her if there were no other woman living."

The young woman from Macy's quite agreed with the Professor, and it was not without satisfaction that she heard him express himself in this manner.

"Well," she continued, "then there is Miss Blagden. She is of a more suitable age."

"The Disagreeable Woman. What do you take me for, Mees Ruth? She is too strong-minded."

"Perhaps so, but I am sure she has a kind heart."

"I should never be happy with her—never!" said the Professor, decidedly.

"Were you ever married, Professor?" asked Ruth with sudden curiosity.

"Yes, I was married when I was thirty—but my Gretchen only lived two years. I haf mourned for her more than thirty years."

"You have waited a long time, Professor."

"Yes; till I saw you, Mees Ruth, I never haf seen the woman I wanted to marry. Perhaps," he added with sudden hope, "this young man, Stephen, does not wish to marry you."

"He will be only too glad," said Ruth, tossing her head. "He offered himself to me a year ago."

"Then there is no hope for me?"

"None at all, Professor."

They had reached Waverly Place, and so there was no time for further conversation. As they came up the stoop Mrs. Wyman saw them through the window. She was in waiting in the hall.

"Have you had a nice walk *together?*" she purred.

"How I hate that woman!" said Ruth to herself.

She ran upstairs and prepared for supper.

CHAPTER SIXTEEN
SITS THE WIND IN THAT QUARTER

Of course I attended the Patti concert. The seat given me was in the best part of the house, and I felt somewhat bashful when I found that all my neighbors wore dress suits. My own suit—the best I had—was beginning to show the marks of wear, but I did not dare go to the expense of another.

My next neighbor was an elderly gentleman, bordering upon sixty. In the twenty minutes that elapsed before the rise of the curtain we fell into a pleasant conversation. It was pleasant to find that he was becoming interested in me.

"You enjoy Patti?" he said. "But then I hardly need ask that. Your presence here is sufficient evidence."

"I have no doubt I shall enjoy Patti," I answered. "I have never heard her."

"Indeed? How does that happen?"

"Because I have been only three months in New York. I came here from the country, and of course I had no chance to hear her there."

"Excuse my curiosity, but you do not look like a businessman."

"I am not. I am a practicing physician."

"Indeed!" he replied, with interest. "I wish you could cure my rheumatism."

"I should like a chance to try."

This was a little audacious, as probably he had his own family physician, but it came naturally upon his remark.

"You shall try," he said, impulsively. "My family physician has failed to benefit me."

"It may be so with me."

"At any rate I will try you. Can you call at my house tomorrow at eleven o'clock?"

"I will do so with pleasure."

He gave me his card. I found that his name was Gregory Vincent, and that he lived in one of the finest parts of Madison Avenue. It occurred to me that he was perhaps imprudent in trusting an unknown young physician, but I was not foolish enough to tell him so.

"I will call," I said with professional gravity, and I entered the name and engagement in my medical notebook.

Here the curtain rose, and our thoughts were soon occupied by the stage.

When the concert was over, my new friend as he shook my hand, said, "I can rely upon your calling tomorrow, Dr. Fenwick?"

"I will not fail you."

"I don't know how it is," he said, "but though we are strangers I have a prophetic instinct that you can help me."

"I will do my best, Mr. Vincent."

Congratulating myself on my new and promising patient, I made my way into the lobby. There presently I met Mrs. Wyman and Count Penelli. I learned later that she had purchased two cheap seats and invited the Count to accompany her. They had not distinguished me in the audience, I was so far away from them.

"Dr. Fenwick!" exclaimed Mrs. Wyman, in surprise. "I thought you said you were not coming."

"I changed my mind," I answered, smiling. "Of course, you enjoyed the concert?"

"Did I not? But where were you sitting?"

"In the orchestra."

"What! Among the millionaires?"

"I don't know if they were millionaires. I was ashamed of my appearance. All wore dress suits except myself and the ladies."

"It seems to me, doctor, you were extravagant."

"It does seem so."

I did not propose to enlighten Mrs. Wyman as to the small expense I was at for a ticket. I could see with secret amusement that her respect for me was increased by my supposed liberal outlay. In this respect I showed to advantage beside her escort who had availed himself of a ticket purchased by her. She had represented that the tickets were sent her by the management.

"The Count had an advantage over us," said the widow. "He could understand the language."

"*Si,* Signora," said the Count, with a smile.

"It wasn't the words I cared for," said I. "I should enjoy Patti if she sang in Arabic."

"Well, perhaps so. Were you ever in Italy, doctor?"

"No, the only foreign country I ever visited was New Jersey."

"Is New Jersey then a foreign country?" asked the Count, puzzled.

"It is only a joke, Count," said the widow.

"And a poor one, I admit."

"The Count had been telling me of his ancestral home, of the vine-clad hills, and the olive trees, and the orange groves. Oh, I am wild to visit that charming Italy."

"Perhaps you may do so some day, my dear Mrs. Wyman," said the Count, in a soft tone.

The widow cast down her eyes.

"It would be too lovely," she said.

When we reached the boarding-house, the Count asked, "May I come up to your room, Dr. Fenwick?"

"Certainly. I shall be glad to have you do so." My room was a small one. I should have had to pay a higher price for a larger one. However, I gave the Count my only chair, and sat on the bed.

"Is it permitted?" he asked, as he lighted a cigarette.

"Oh, yes," I replied, but I only said so out of politeness. It was decidedly disagreeable to have any one smoke in my chamber in the evening. I could, however, open the window afterwards and give it an airing.

"Mrs. Wyman is a very fine woman," said the Count, after a pause.

"Very," I responded, briefly.

"And she is rich, is she not?" he asked, in some anxiety.

"Sits the wind in that quarter?" I thought. "Well, I won't stand in the way."

"She seems independent."

"Ah! you mean——"

"That she has enough to live upon. She never seemed to have any money troubles. I suppose it is the same with you, you no doubt draw a revenue from your estates in Italy?"

"No, no, you make a mistake. They belong to my father, and he is displease with me. He will send me no money."

"Are you the oldest son?"

"*Si*, Signor!" but he answered hesitatingly.

"Then you will be all right some day."

"True, doctor, some day, but just now I am what you call short. You could do me a great favor."

"What is it?"

"If you could lend me fifty dollar?"

"My dear Count, it would be quite impossible. Do you think I am rich?"

"You pay five—six dollar for your ticket to hear Patti."

"It was imprudent, but I wished to hear her; now I must be careful."

"I would pay you when I get my next remittance from Italy."

"It will not be possible," I answered, firmly. "Have you asked Prof. Poppendorf?"

"No! Has he got money?"

"I think he has more than I."

"I have a special use for the money," said the Count, but I did not ask what it was.

Presently the Count rose and left me. It took twenty minutes to clear the room of the vile smell of cigarette smoke.

"After all," thought I, "there is a chance for Mrs. Wyman to become a Countess, that is if he is a real Count." Upon this point I did not feel certain.

"Well, did you enjoy Patti?" asked Miss Blagden at the breakfast table.

"Immensely. Why did you not go?"

"Because I have very little taste for music," answered the Disagreeable Woman.

"Mrs. Wyman was there."

"She sings," said Miss Blagden, with a slight smile.

"Yes, the Count was with her."

"Humph! where did they sit?"

"In the upper part of the house somewhere. I felt myself out of place among the Four Hundred. But it brought me luck."

"How is that?"

"I secured a patient, a Mr. Gregory Vincent of Madison Avenue."

"Was Gregory Vincent there? How did you make his acquaintance?"

"He was my next neighbor. He seemed to take a liking to me, confided to me that he was a victim of rheumatism, and I am to assume charge of his case."

"I am very glad," said Miss Blagden, heartily. "Do your best to cure him."

"I will."

"And don't be afraid to send him in a good bill."

"I am sure he will pay me liberally."

"It may be your stepping stone to success."

"Thank you for your kind interest."

"And how is your poor patient—Alice Mills?"

"Quite well now, but I wish she were not obliged to spend so many hours in a crowded store."

"When do you call there again?"

"I may call this morning."

"I will go with you. I have a plan for them."

Miss Blagden accompanied me to the poor house. She was so kind and gentle that I did not understand how any one could call her the Disagreeable Woman.

In a few days, thanks to her, Mrs. Mills was installed as housekeeper to a wealthy widower in Fifty-seventh Street. Alice was made governess to two young children, and Frank was provided with a home in return for some slight services.

CHAPTER SEVENTEEN
MY RICH PATIENT

When I was admitted to the house of Gregory Vincent, I was surprised by its magnificence. It has been said that there are few palaces in Europe that compare in comfort and luxury with a first class New York mansion. I have never been in a palace, and Mr. Vincent's house was the only aristocratic house which I had had an opportunity to view. But I am prepared to indorse the remark.

I handed my card to the liveried servant who opened the door.

"Dr. Fenwick," he repeated. "Yes, sir; you are expected."

He led me upstairs into an elegant library, or sitting-room and library combined. Here sat my acquaintance of the evening before, with his foot swathed in bandages and resting on a chair, while he was seated in a cosy arm-chair.

"Good-morning, doctor," he said. "I am glad to see you. You see that I am in the grasp of my old enemy."

"We will try to rout him," I said, cheerfully.

"That sounds well, and encourages me. Do you know, Dr. Fenwick, that without any special reason I feel great confidence in you. You are a young man, probably not more than half as old as my regular physician, but he has not been able to do me any good."

"And I hope to be able to do so."

"I suppose you have had experience in such cases?"

"Yes, I have an old aunt who had suffered untold tortures from rheumatism. She put herself under my charge, and for her sake I made an extensive study of rheumatic cases and remedies."

"Well?" he asked, eagerly.

"I finally cured her. It is now three years since she has had a twinge."

"Good! My instinct was correct. That gives me hopes of success under your charge. Don't be afraid to lose your patient by effecting a speedy cure. I will make you a promise. When you have so far cured me that I am free from rheumatic pains for three months, I will hand you a check for a thousand dollars."

"A thousand dollars!" I repeated with sparkling eyes. "That will indeed be an inducement."

"Of course I shall pay you your regular fees besides."

I could hardly credit my good fortune. I was like one who had just received intelligence that I had drawn a large sum in the lottery. I determined to win the promised check if there was any chance.

I began to question Mr. Vincent as to his trouble. I found that it was a case of rheumatic gout. A difficult case, but very similar to that of my aunt. I resolved to try the same treatment with him.

I wished to ask some questions, but he forestalled them.

"I have no wife," he said. "I was left a widower many years ago. My niece and myself constitute our whole family."

"Don't you feel lonely at times?" I asked.

"Yes. My niece has her friends, suited to one of her age, but little company for me. If I had a nephew now—like yourself—it would cheer me up and give me a new interest in life."

"I wish you were my uncle," I said to myself.

"I am an old man, but I have great interest in young company. I think it was that that drew me toward you at Patti's concert. When I learned that you were a physician I saw that I could make it worth your while to call on an old man. I hope you are not a very busy man."

"Not yet," I answered, guardedly. I felt that it would be unwise to let him know how far from a busy man I was.

"Then you will be able to call upon me every day."

"I will do so gladly, but it will not be necessary—from a medical point of view."

"No matter! I shall be glad to have you come, and of course I pay for your time. It will be an advantage, no doubt, to have your patient under constant observation."

"That is true."

"Now I won't put you to the trouble of keeping an account of your visits. I will agree to pay you twenty-five dollars a week if that will be satisfactory."

Twenty-five dollars a week! Why I scarcely made that sum in fees in a month.

"It is more than I should think of charging," I said, frankly.

"Then it is satisfactory. Your money will be paid you at the end of every week."

When I left the house I felt as if I had suddenly come into a fortune. Now I could see my way clear. The little stock of money which still remained to me would suffer no further diminution. On the contrary, I should be able to add to it.

It is said that there comes to every man once in his life a chance to succeed. Apparently mine had come to me, and this chance had come to me through the Disagreeable Woman.

CHAPTER EIGHTEEN
THE PROFESSOR'S BOOK

For some weeks matters went on quietly at our boarding-house. Prof. Poppendorf, in spite of the failure of his matrimonial schemes, ate, smoked, and drank as tranquilly as ever. Ruth was grateful to him that he had accepted her refusal as final, and disturbed her no more. They still sat near each other at the table, but there was never anything in his manner to indicate that there had been any romantic passages between them.

The Disagreeable Woman remained as great a mystery as ever. Sometimes she was absent for three or four days together. Then she would suddenly reappear. No one ever asked where she had been. It would have taken rare courage to do that. Nor did she ever volunteer any explanation.

Whether she possessed large means or not no one could conjecture. She always paid her board bill, and with unfailing regularity, at the end of every week. Her dress was always plain, but oftentimes of costly material. She seldom indulged in conversation, though she was always ready with an answer when spoken to. Perhaps I may mention as exceptions to her general rule of reticence the young woman from Macy's and myself. She seemed to feel more kindly toward us than toward any of the others.

There had been various attempts to find out where she lived. None had succeeded. One day Mrs. Wyman asked the question directly.

"Where do you live, Miss Blagden, if you will allow me to ask?"

"I will allow you to ask," returned the Disagreeable Woman, coolly. "Do you propose to call on me?"

"If you will permit me."

"It is hardly necessary. We meet at the table every day. I am a hermit," she added after a pause, "I do not care to receive visitors."

"I once heard of a hermit who lived in one of the cottages on the rocks near Central Park," said the widow, rather impertinently.

"I don't live there!" said the Disagreeable Woman, composedly.

"Of course not. I did not suppose you did."

"Thank you. You are right as usual."

If Miss Blagden meant to be sarcastic, nothing in her tone revealed it. She had warded off the attack dictated by curiosity.

Whether Miss Blagden was rich or not, she was always ready to contribute to any public or private cause. When Prof. Poppendorf announced that he was about to publish a book, enlarged from his lecture on "The Material and The Immaterial," Miss Blagden subscribed for two copies.

"One is for you, Dr. Fenwick!" she said, in a low tone.

"Thank you, Miss Blagden. You are very kind. Am I expected to read it?"

"If you can," she responded with a grim smile.

The other boarders were asked, but each had some excuse.

"I have just bought a new hat," said Mrs. Wyman.

"I no understand English," said the Count.

"Do you think I ought to subscribe, Miss Blagden?" asked Ruth.

"No, child. Why should you? You have a use for your money. Besides, you would not understand it. If you wish, I will buy one for you?"

"No, thank you, Miss Blagden. It would be of no use to me, but I thought the Professor would think it friendly."

She could not explain that she wished to make amends for refusing his suit, for she had with rare delicacy abstained from mentioning the learned German's uncouth courtship. Perhaps Miss Blagden, who was very observing, penetrated her motive, for she said: "There is something in that. Subscribe, and I will pay for the book."

Upon this Ruth gently told the Professor that she would take a copy.

He was surprised and delighted.

"By all means Mees Ruth, but perhaps I should give you one."

"No, no, Prof. Poppendorf. I want to show my interest in you—and your book."

"You are so good. I will give you the first copy."

"Thank you," said Ruth, shyly.

"What do you want of the old fossil's book?" asked Mrs. Wyman later, when the Professor was out of hearing. "I suspect that you are in love with the Professor."

"No, you don't suspect that," said Ruth, composedly.

"At any rate he seems struck with you."

"I suppose I am either material or immaterial," returned Ruth, laughing.

"You went to walk with him one evening."

"I am afraid you are jealous, Mrs. Wyman."

The widow laughed and the conversation ended.

CHAPTER NINETEEN
A SPEECH FROM THE THRONE

It was some time since Mrs. Gray had made any communication to the boarders.

But one evening she seemed laboring under suppressed excitement.

"Something is up," said Mr. Blake, the young reporter who sat on my left, the Disagreeable Woman being on my right.

"We shall have it after supper," I answered.

Mrs. Gray always waited till the last boarder had finished his meal. It was one of the unwritten laws of the boarding-house.

The last boarder on this occasion was Professor Poppendorf. He was the heartiest eater, and we usually had to wait for him. When he had taken the last sip of beer, for in consideration of his national tastes he was always supplied with a schooner of that liquid which is dear to the Teutonic heart, Mrs. Gray opened her mouth.

"My friends," she said, "I have a letter to read to you."

She opened a perfumed billet, adjusted her spectacles, and read.

"It is from Mrs. Wyman," she said, "and it is at her request that I read it."

We had already noticed that neither Mrs. Wyman nor the Count was present.

Mrs. Gray began:

> "My Dear Mrs. Gray:
>
> For three years I have been an inmate of your happy home. I have come to feel an interest in it and in all whose acquaintance I have made here. I had no thought of leaving you, but circumstances make it necessary. Let me say at once that I have consented to marry Count di Penelli. You who are familiar with his fine traits and aristocratic bearing will hardly be surprised that I have been unable to resist his ardent entreaties. I had indeed intended never to marry again, but it was because I never expected to find one who could take the place of my dear departed first husband. The Count and I leave by an early train for Philadelphia where the ceremony will be performed. We may remain there for a few days. Beyond that our plans are not arranged. We would have had a public wedding and invited our friends, but as the Count's family are in Italy and cannot be present, we thought it best to have a simple private ceremony. When we go to Italy next summer there may be another ceremony at the Penelli Castle in Southern Italy.
>
> "I cannot tell when I shall return to New York. Probably I shall never again be an inmate of your happy home. The Count and I may take a flat up-town—a whole house would be too large for us. But I shall—we shall certainly call on our old friends, and I trust that the ties that bind us together in friendship may never weaken.
>
> "I shall soon be the Countess di Penelli. But once more and for the last time, I subscribe myself
>
> "Your faithful and devoted
>
> "Letitia Wyman"

We listened to the reading of the letter in silent excitement. Then there was a chorus of exclamations.

"Did you ever?" ejaculated the young woman from Macy's.

"I am not surprised," said the Disagreeable Woman, calmly. "Mrs. Wyman has been courting the Count ever since he came here."

"You mean that he has been paying his attentions to her," suggested Mr. Blake, the reporter.

"No, I mean what I say."

"She says she had no thought of marrying again."

"Mr. Blake, you are a young man. You don't understand women, and particularly widows. Probably there is not a gentleman at the table whom Mrs. Wyman has not thought of as a matrimonial subject, yourself not excepted."

Mr. Blake was a very young man, and he blushed.

"She would not have married me," growled the Professor.

Most of us smiled.

"Are you pledged to celibacy, Professor?" asked the landlady.

"No, madam. If a certain young lady would marry me I would marry tomorrow."

Ruth Canby blushed furiously, and was indignant with herself for doing so, especially as it drew all glances to her.

"Let us hope you may be successful in your suit, Professor," said Mrs. Gray.

"Thank you, my dear lady; time will show."

Miss Blagden turned her searching glance upon the flaming cheeks of Ruth and smiled kindly. If there was any one at the table whom she liked it was the young woman from Macy's.

"I suppose there is no doubt about his being a Count," suggested Mr. Blake.

"I should say there was a good deal of doubt," answered the Disagreeable Woman.

"Do you really think so?"

"It is my conjecture."

"Oh, I think there is no doubt about it," said the landlady, who prided herself on having had so aristocratic a boarder.

"I am a loser by this marriage," said Mrs. Gray. "I have two rooms suddenly vacated."

"A friend of mine will take one of them," said Mr. Blake, the reporter. "He has been wishing to get in here for a month."

"I shall be glad to receive him," said Mrs. Gray, graciously.

The other room was also taken within a week.

CHAPTER TWENTY
A STARTLING DISCOVERY

Usually I secured a morning paper, and ran over the contents at my office while waiting for patients.

It was perhaps a week later that I selected the *Herald*—I did not confine myself exclusively to one paper—and casually my eye fell upon the arrivals at the hotels.

I started in surprise as I read among the guests at the Brevoort House the name of Count di Penelli.

"What!" I exclaimed, "are our friends back again? Why is not the Countess mentioned? Perhaps, however, the Count has left his wife in Philadelphia, and come on here on business."

It chanced that I had occasion to pass the Brevoort an hour later.

I was prompted to call and inquire for the Count.

"Yes, he is in. Will you send up your card?"

I hastily inscribed my name on a card and sent it up to his room.

The bell-boy soon returned.

"The Count will be glad to see you, sir," he said. "Will you follow me?"

"He is getting ceremonious," I reflected. "I thought he would come down to see me."

I followed the bell-boy to a room on the second floor.

"Dr. Fenwick?" he said, as the door was opened.

I saw facing me a tall, slender, dark-complexioned man of about forty-five, a perfect stranger to me.

"I wished to see Count di Penelli," I stammered, in some confusion.

"I am the Count," he answered, courteously.

"But the Count I know is a young man."

"There is no other Count di Penelli."

"Pardon me!" I said, "but a young man calling himself by that name was for two months a fellow boarder of mine."

"Describe him, if you please," said the Count, eagerly.

I did so.

"Ah," said the Count, when I concluded, "it is doubtless my valet, who has been masquerading under my title. He ran away from me at the West, nearly three months since, carrying with him three hundred dollars. I set detectives upon his track, but they could find no clue. Is the fellow still at your boarding-house?"

"No, Count, he eloped a week since with a widow, another of our boarders. I believe they are in Philadelphia."

"Then he has deceived the poor woman. Has she got money?"

"A little. I don't think she has much."

"That is what he married her for. Doubtless he supposed her wealthy. He had probably spent all the money he took from me."

"I hope, Count, for the sake of his wife, you will not have him arrested."

Count di Penelli shrugged his shoulders.

"I will let him go at your request, poor devil," he said. "Why did she marry him?"

"For his title."

"Then the heart is not concerned?"

"I never discovered that Mrs. Wyman had a heart."

"Probably both will be heartily sick of the marriage, perhaps are so already."

"Thank you for your information, Count."

"And I thank you for yours. Good-morning!"

I said nothing at the boarding-house of the discovery I had made. Why should I? So far as the rest of the boarders knew Mrs. Wyman was a veritable Countess.

CHAPTER TWENTY-ONE
AFTER THREE MONTHS

The curtain falls and rises again after an interval of three months.

There have been some changes in our boarding-house. Prof. Poppendorf still occupies his accustomed place, and so does Miss Blagden. The young reporter still sits at my left, and entertains me with interesting gossip and information about public affairs and public men with whom he has come in contact.

But the young woman from Macy's has left us. She has returned to her country home and is now the wife of her rustic admirer, Stephen Higgins. I think she has done wisely. Life in the great stores is a species of slavery, and she could save nothing from her salary. When Prof.

Poppendorf heard of her marriage, he looked depressed, but I noticed that his appetite was not affected. A true Teuton seldom allows anything to interfere with that.

Mrs. Gray has received two or three notes from the Countess di Penelli. They treated of business matters solely. Whether she has discovered that her husband's title is spurious I cannot tell. I hear, however, from a drummer who is with us at intervals, that she is keeping a boarding-house on Spring Garden Street, and that her title has been the magnet that has drawn to her house many persons who are glad in this way to obtain a titled acquaintance.

As for myself I am on the high road to a comfortable income. I was fortunate enough to give my rich patient so much relief that I have received the large check he promised me, and have been recommended by him to several of his friends. I have thought seriously of removing to a more fashionable neighborhood, but have refrained—will it be believed?—from my reluctance to leave the Disagreeable Woman. I am beginning to understand her better. Under a brusque exterior she certainly possesses a kind heart, and consideration for others. Upon everything in the shape of humbug or pretension she is severe, but she can appreciate worth and true nobility. In more than one instance I have applied to her in behalf of a poor patient, and never in vain.

Yet I am as much in the dark as ever as to her circumstances and residence. Upon these subjects I have ceased, not perhaps to feel, but to show any curiosity. The time was coming, however, when I should learn more of her.

One day a young girl came to my office. Her mother kept a modest lodging house on West Eleventh Street, and she had been my patient.

"Any one sick at home, Sarah?" I asked.

"No, doctor, but we have a lodger who is very low with a fever. I think he is very poor. I am afraid he cannot pay a doctor, but mother thought you would be willing to call."

"To be sure," I said, cheerfully, "I will be at your house in an hour."

An hour found me ringing at the door of Mrs. Graham's plain lodging house.

"I thought you would come, Dr. Fenwick," said the good woman, who personally answered the bell. "You come in good time, for poor Mr. Douglas is very sick."

"I will follow you to his room."

He occupied a small room on the third floor. It was furnished in plain fashion. The patient, a man who was apparently nearing fifty, was tossing restlessly on his bed. Poorly situated as he was, I could see that in health he must have been a man of distinguished bearing. Poverty and he seemed ill-mated.

"Mr. Douglas," said the landlady, "this is Dr. Fenwick. I took the liberty of calling him, as you are so ill."

The sick man turned upon me a glance from a pair of full, black eyes.

"Dr. Fenwick," he said, sadly, "I thank you for coming, but I am almost a pauper, and I fear I cannot pay you for your services."

"That matters little," I replied. "You need me, that is enough. Let me feel your pulse."

I found that he was in a high fever. His symptoms were serious. He looked like a man with a constitution originally strong, but it had been severely tried."

"Well?" he asked.

"You are seriously ill. I am not prepared just now with my diagnosis, but I can tell better in a day or two."

"Shall I be long ill?" he asked.

"It will take time to recover."

"Shall I recover?" he asked, pointedly.

"We will hope for the best."

"I understand. Don't think I am alarmed. Life has few charms for me. My chief trouble is that I shall be a burden to you and Mrs. Graham."

"Don't think of me, I have a fair practice, but I have time for you."

"Thank you, doctor. You are very kind."

"Let me put down your name," I said, taking down my tablets.

"My name is Philip Douglas."

I noted the name, and shortly left him.

I felt that in his critical condition he ought to have a nurse, but where was the money to come from to pay one?

"He is no common man," I reflected. "He has been rich. His personal surroundings do not fit him."

Somehow I had already come to feel an interest in my patient. There was something in his appearance that set me wondering what his past could have been.

"It must have been his misfortune, not his fault," I decided, for he bore no marks of dissipation.

Under favorable circumstances I felt that I could pull him through, but without careful attendance and generous living there was great doubt. What should I do? I decided to speak of his case to the Disagreeable Woman.

CHAPTER TWENTY-TWO
I APPEAL TO THE DISAGREEABLE WOMAN

"Miss Blagden," I said when the opportunity came, "I want to interest you in a patient of mine—a gentleman to whom I was called this morning."

"Speak freely, doctor. Is there anything I can do for him?"

"Much, for he requires much. He is lying in a poor lodging-house grievously ill with a fever. He has little or no money, yet he must once have been in affluent circumstances. Without a trained nurse, and the comforts that only money can buy, I fear he will not live."

"It is a sad case. I am willing to cooperate with you. What is your patient's name?"

"Philip Douglas."

"Philip Douglas!" she exclaimed, in evident excitement. "Tell me quickly, what is his appearance?"

"He is a large man, of sriking appearance, with full, dark eyes, who must in earlier days have been strikingly handsome."

"And he is poor, and ill?" she said, breathless.

"Very poor and very ill."

Her breath came quick. She seemed deeply agitated.

"And where is he living?"

"In No. — West Eleventh Street."

"Take me there at once."

I looked at her in amazement.

"Dr. Fenwick," she said, "you wonder at my excitement. I will explain it. This man, Philip Douglas, and I were once engaged to be married. The engagement was broken through my fault and my folly. I have regretted it many times. I have much to answer for. I fear that I wrecked his life, and it may be too late to atone. But I will try. Lead me to him."

I bowed gravely, and we set out.

Arriving at the lodging-house I thought it prudent to go up alone. I feared that excitement might be bad for my patient.

He was awake and resting more comfortably.

"How do you feel?" I asked.

"Better, doctor. Thanks to you."

"Have you no relatives whom you would wish to see—or friends?"

"I have no relatives in New York," he said.

"Or friends?"

He paused and looked thoughtful.

"I don't know," he answered, slowly. "There is one—I have not seen her for many years—but it is impossible, yet I would give my life to see Jane Blagden."

"Why not send for her?"

"She would not come. We were friends once—very dear friends—I hoped to marry her. Now I am poor and broken in health, I must give up the thought."

"Could you bear to see her? Would it not make you ill?"

"What do you mean, doctor?" he asked, quickly.

"I mean that Miss Blagden is below. She wishes to see you."

"Can it be? Are you a magician? How could you know of her?"

"Never mind that. Shall I bring her up?"

"Yes."

CHAPTER TWENTY-THREE
AT LAST

Jane Blagden paused a moment at the entrance to the room, as if to gather strength for the interview. I had never seen her so moved. Then she opened the door and entered with a firm step.

He lay on the bed with his eyes fixed eagerly on the door. As she entered he tried to raise his head.

"Jane!" he exclaimed, eagerly.

She placed her hand for a moment on her heart, as if to still its throbbing. Then she walked quickly to the bed.

"Philip!" she said.

"At last!" he cried, in a low voice.

"Can you forgive me, Philip, dear Philip?"

"If there is anything to forgive."

"There is—much. I am afraid you have suffered."

"I have."

"And so have I. Since we parted I have been lonely—desolate. I let my pride and my obstinacy come between us—but I have been punished."

She had drawn a chair to the bed-side, and sitting down took his hand in hers. It was hot, feverish.

"You are very ill, I fear."

"I shall be better now," he murmured. "It is worth much to have you beside me."

I looked at the face of the Disagreeable Woman. I saw upon it an expression I had never seen before—an expression that made her look ten years younger. I could not have believed in the tenderness, the heart-warmth which it showed.

"Philip," she said, "you must get well for my sake."

"And if I do?" he asked, eagerly.

"It shall be as you wish."

He closed his eyes, and a look of happiness and content lighted up his features. But soon there was a change. It was evident that the excitement had been too much for him."

"Miss Blagden," I said, "I think you must go. Our patient is too weak to stand any more excitement or agitation."

"Can I not stay here as his nurse?" she pleaded.

"It will be better to have a trained nurse—one who will not agitate him."

"As you think best, doctor," she said, meekly, "but I will stay in the house. How soon can you send a nurse?"

"Within an hour."

"Do so, and I will stay here till then. If he wakes I will leave the room."

Within an hour a trained nurse was installed in the sick chamber. Miss Blagden made an arrangement with Mrs. Graham to occupy a room which had fortunately been vacated the day previous. It was small and uncomfortable, but she cared little for this.

CHAPTER TWENTY-FOUR
THE LIGHT OF HOPE

Then commenced the struggle with disease. Philip Douglas was very ill. I had not exaggerated the danger. He was unconscious most of the time, but in spite of that he seemed to have a dim consciousness that there was some good in store for him.

While he was unconscious Miss Blagden felt at liberty to spend a part of her time in the room. She assisted the nurse, and waited patiently for the patient's amendment.

For three days it was a matter of doubt whether he would live or die. I gave up all other patients for him. I had become almost as anxious as Miss Blagden. I watched Philip Douglas narrowly to note any change either for the better or worse. It was a long and wearisome vigil. I was waiting for the crisis.

At length it came. He began to breathe more freely, though still unconscious. I noticed a change for the better in his pulse. Her eyes as well as mine were fixed upon the sick man. Finally her eyes sought my face with eager questioning.

"Is there a change?" she asked.

"Yes, he will live."

"Thank God!" she breathed, fervently, and a look of grateful joy lighted up the face of the Disagreeable Woman.

Index

Alger, Horatio, Jr.
  adult novels of, 16–19
  biography of, 1–2
  formula of, 3–4
  homosexual controversy concerning, 7–15
  influence of, 4–7
Alger, A Biography Without A Hero (Mayes), 12
Allen, Frederick Lewis, 6
American Idea of Success, The (Huber), 12–13
American Opinion (magazine), 14
American Quarterly (journal), 15
Andersen, Hans Christian, 3
Argosy (magazine), 17
Atkinson, Brooks, 7

Behrman, S. N., 7, 16, 17
Birmingham, Stephen, 13
Blanck, Jacob, 6
Boston Herald (newspaper), 11
Broun, Heywood, 7
Bullough, Vern L., 14–15
Bully of the Village, The (Alger), 4

Cape Cod's Way (Corbett), 7
Cardozo, Benjamin, 13
Carleton, G. W., 17
Cheney, Amos Parker, 11
Corbett, Scott, 7
Cowley, Malcolm, 6
Crotty, Ken, 11
Crouse, Russel, 6, 7

Detroit Free Press (newspaper), 13
Dickens, Charles, 3
Dillingham, G. W., 17, 18
Dime Novel Roundup (Pachon), 16
Disagreeable Woman, The (Alger), 17, 18
DiSalle, Michael V., 5
Dixon, Franklin W. (Leslie McFarlane), 14
Donahue, M. A., 6

Einstein, Lewis, 13
Evans, Medford, 14

Fairless, Benjamin, 5
Fame and Fortune (Alger), 6
Fancy of Hers, A (Alger), 16, 17
Farley, James A., 5
Fiction Factory, The (Reynolds), 6
Fitzgerald, F. Scott, 5, 19
From Rags to Riches (Tebbel), 12

Gallico, Paul, 4

Ghost of the Hardy Boys (McFarlane), 14
Golden Multitudes (Mott), 6
Grandees, The (Birmingham), 13
Great Gatsby, The (Fitzgerald), 19
Grimm, Jakob Ludwig Karl and Wilhelm Karl, 3
Grolier Club, 6
Gruber, Frank, 6

Hardy Boys stories (Dixon), 14
Hellman, Geoffrey T., 13
Hemingway, Ernest, 5
Henderson, Bill, 12
Holbrook, Stewart H., 6, 7
homosexual controversy, 2, 7–15
Homosexuality: A History (Bullough), 14–15
Horatio Alger, Jr. (Gruber), 6
Horatio Alger: or, The American Hero Era (Gardner), 5, 7, 18
Horatio's Boys (Hoyt), 6, 14
Hoyt, Edwin P., 6, 14
Huber, Richard M., 12–13

Jack's Ward (Alger), 16

Kilmer, Joyce, 5

Lehman, Herbert H., 13
Longfellow, Henry Wadsworth, 2
Loring, A. K., 4–5, 16, 17
Lost Men of American History (Holbrook), 6
Luck and Pluck (Alger), 6

Mathewson, Christy, 5
Mayes, Herbert R., 12
McFarlane, Leslie, 14
Moby Dick (Melville), 6
Mott, Frank Luther, 6
Munsey, Frank A., 17, 18
Munsey's Magazine, 17, 18

New Republic, The, 6
Newsboy's Lodging House, 12, 15
New Schoolma'am, The; or, A Summer in North Sparta (Alger), 17
Newsweek (magazine), 13
New York Sun (newspaper), 16
New York Times (newspaper), 7, 12
New York Times Book Review, 13, 15
New York Times Magazine, 6
Nye, Russel, 15

O'Brien, Frank M., 16
O'Connor, Charles, 12
Our Crowd (Birmingham), 13

Pachon, Stanley, 16
Pacific Series (Alger), 17
Parmenter, Mabel, 11
Pegler, Westbrook, 7
Peter Parley to Penrod (Blanck), 6
Porter & Coates, 18
Preston, Charles F. (Alger pseudonym), 16
Publishers Weekly, 12

Ragged Dick (Alger), 2, 4, 6
Resources in American Literary Studies, 15
Reston, James, 5
Reynolds, Quentin, 6, 16
Road to Success, The (Gardner), 18
Rockne, Knute, 5

Salisbury, Harrison E., 12
Sandburg, Carl, 5
Saturday Review of Literature, The, 6
Seelye, John, 15
Seligman, Joseph, 13

Smith, Alfred E., 5
Spellman, Francis Cardinal, 5
Starr, Julian (Alger pseudonym), 18
Story of the Sun, The (O'Brien), 16
Strive and Succeed (Behrman), 7
Struggling Upward and Other Works (Crouse), 6

Tattered Tom (Alger), 6
Tebbel, John, 12
Timothy Crump's Ward (Alger), 16
Tom Tracy (Alger), 19

Uncle Tom's Cabin (Stowe), 6
Uniteen News (magazine), 10

Wait and Hope (Alger), 17
Washington Star (newspaper), 13

Young Miner, The (Alger), 15